Gemma

exasperated by him

"You certainly don't think much of me, do you?"
she asked.

"Not true," Chad replied. "When you get to know
me better, you'll see that I don't bother much with
people I don't care about. Let alone charging to
their rescue."

When you get to know me better . . . Gemma felt a
funny little quiver run through her. Did he want to
know her better? Did she want to get to know him
better?

You could be playing with fire here, Gemma Hayes,
she warned herself. Do you honestly think you
could go on seeing this man and remain indifferent
to him? You need that kind of complication like a
hole in the head! Think of your future . . .
your career!

Elizabeth Duke says that her main interest and love is writing, although she's awfully fond of traveling, too. She's visited almost every state in her native Australia and has traveled to New Zealand, the U.S., Canada and Mexico, which leaves her with no shortage of fascinating settings for her romance novels. The author is married and has two children.

Books by Elizabeth Duke

HARLEQUIN ROMANCE
2833—SOFTLY FLITS A SHADOW

Don't miss any of our special offers. Write to us at the following address for information on our newest releases.

Harlequin Reader Service
901 Fuhrmann Blvd., P.O. Box 1397, Buffalo, NY 14240
Canadian address: P.O. Box 603,
Fort Erie, Ont. L2A 5X3

Island
Deception
Elizabeth Duke

Harlequin Books

TORONTO • NEW YORK • LONDON
AMSTERDAM • PARIS • SYDNEY • HAMBURG
STOCKHOLM • ATHENS • TOKYO • MILAN

Original hardcover edition published in 1989
by Mills & Boon Limited

ISBN 0-373-03034-7

Harlequin Romance first edition February 1990

CHAPTER ONE

GEMMA was strolling towards the island resort's palm-fringed swimming pool when she first noticed the woman standing by the poolside. The woman was conspicuous among the half-naked bodies lounging around the pool because she was fully dressed. Eye-catchingly so, in a gorgeous rainbow-coloured silk dress adorned with frills and ruffles. Though exquisitely designed, it struck Gemma as being rather incongruous attire for a poolside, particularly in this heat and humidity.

The second thing Gemma noticed about the woman was that she was watching her—and making no secret of it.

The towel Gemma had carelessly slung over her shoulder provided scant cover, and, feeling vaguely uncomfortable under the woman's steady appraisal, she turned her back on her, wishing now that she had worn a shirt or a wrap of some kind over her skimpy red bikini.

Finding a vacant lounge-chair, she threw down her towel, kicked off her shoes, and strolled to the edge of the pool. Before diving into the shimmering blue water, curiosity prompted her to flick a look round. The woman in the ruffled dress was still watching her, idly tapping her chin with a well-manicured finger and chewing on her lip as if, Gemma thought indignantly, she was sizing her up for the meat market.

She stood hesitating a moment at the edge of the pool, for virtually the first time in her life feeling self-conscious. She was tempted to grab her towel and sprint back to her Polynesian-style bure, the thatched-hut cottage that was the usual tourist accommodation, and stay there until she was sure the woman had gone. But why should she? She felt a flare of rebellion. Why should she run away and hide as if her body was something to be ashamed of? She was proud of her body, of her narrow waist and slim hips, her long, shapely legs and her clear skin, already a glowing golden brown after less than two full days on the Great Barrier Reef.

Who *was* that woman?

Maybe she's a white slave trader, Gemma thought facetiously, and for a moment she stared boldly back. As she took in the woman's features—the patrician nose, the wide-set black eyes, the raven-black hair that looked as if it had been scraped back from her rather angular face—Gemma's eyes narrowed, her memory stirring. She had seen that woman's picture somewhere. In the social pages? In a fashion magazine? She had seen it more than once, and had seen it again, only recently.

Then she remembered. It had been in the morning newspaper just the other day. In the Australia Day honours . . . yes, of course! For services to the fashion industry . . . that was it. She was Zara Magatelli, the Australian fashion designer!

Gemma felt a giggle bubbling inside her. Why would the great Magatelli be interested in a young tourist wearing nothing more fashionable than a borrowed resort towel and a tiny piece of red cloth?

Unless she was on the lookout for potential fashion models . . . Gemma almost chuckled aloud at the thought. The woman would be in for a surprise if she learned what Gemma really did for a living!

Pushing Zara Magatelli from her mind, she dived into the cool blue water, and struck out across the pool with even, graceful strokes. She had always loved swimming—just as she loved water sports: surfing, waterskiing, windsurfing, snorkelling, sailing. Any leisure time she had managed to grab over the past six or seven years had been spent—and savoured—on or in the water. Blowing the cobwebs away . . . the cobwebs of long hours of study, and even longer hours working in a challenging and demanding profession.

When she finally left the pool, her bronzed skin gleaming and her fine, silvery-blonde hair clinging to her tanned cheeks, she saw that Zara Magatelli had taken a seat at a poolside table—and that she was still watching her!

Gemma frowned faintly. This was ridiculous! What did Zara Magatelli see in her that she found so fascinating?

She wasn't surprised when the woman rose and approached her.

'Zara Magatelli,' the woman said, holding out a well-manicured hand dripping with gold bracelets. 'Please call me Zara.'

'I'm Gemma Hayes.' Whatever she has in mind, Gemma thought, dabbing at her face with her towel, she's going to be disappointed!

'I must apologise for staring at you, my dear. But I'm hoping you might be able to help me out of a desperate situation.'

Gemma's brown eyes widened. This was a new approach, if the woman was merely on the lookout for new talent!

'Desperate?' she echoed cautiously, disappearing for a moment under her towel to vigorously rub her hair.

Zara waited until she emerged. 'I don't know if you're aware but we're holding a big fashion parade here this evening.'

Gemma's brow rose. Did Zara want her to help in some way behind the scenes? To fetch and carry, help the models dress, that sort of thing?

'I had heard something about it,' she admitted. And I intended to avoid it, she added under her breath. Fashion parades at resorts like this were aimed at the idle, not at the likes of Gemma Hayes, who could barely afford to come to the Whitsunday Islands in the first place, and who had no wish to be tempted into buying wildly glamorous Zara Magatelli fashions that she would seldom, if ever, have a chance to wear.

'I've just had some shattering news,' Zara told her, assuming a suitably shattered expression. 'One of our models for this evening has taken ill and it's too late to fly a replacement up here now, even if I could find a suitable girl at such late notice. My dear, have you ever done any modelling?'

Gemma blinked. 'No. Never.' And never wanted to, what's more, she added under her breath.

'I'm surprised. You move so well . . . you're a natural. And you have a model's figure . . . and the looks of an angel. Exquisite face, divine brown eyes, heavenly blonde hair. What *do* you do for a living? Are you an actress? Or a TV star, perhaps?'

Gemma laughed. 'Far from it. I'm a——' She hesitated. She'd come up here to forget about work, to forget about the traumas of the past weeks, to get away from it all for two glorious weeks. She wasn't in the mood to talk about her work or anything else just now.

'Don't tell me you're someone famous travelling incognito?' Zara Magatelli's dismayed voice filled the silence.

Gemma shook her head, and laughed again. 'It's nothing like that. It's just that I'm here on holiday and I don't even want to think about . . . about what I do back home.' Looking at Zara's puzzled face, she came to a quick decision. 'I'm a doctor,' she explained, relenting.

This was greeted with the usual reaction.

'*What*! You? A doctor? I don't believe it! Why, you look far too young for a start . . .'

'I'm nearly twenty-six,' Gemma said with a smile. 'I qualified two years ago.'

'But—what on earth made you decide to become a *doctor*, darling?' Zara shook her head, curiosity for the moment overriding her desperation. 'With your looks, you could have——'

Gemma had heard all this before. She broke in gently.

'My father is a doctor, and my grandfather and my uncle are doctors too. So medicine is pretty much in my blood. My three older sisters all chose other careers, which meant that everyone looked to me to carry on the family tradition. It wasn't a difficult choice—I've never wanted to do anything else but medicine.'

'Well . . . so you're a doctor.' Zara's black eyes gleamed. 'Then you'll be interested to hear that the proceeds from tonight's parade will be going towards Dr Rivers' new surgery. Do you know him? Dr Chad Rivers. They say he's an excellent doctor. Loads of experience, and very highly respected. He gave up a thriving practice to come there. The resort is lucky to have him.'

Gemma shook her head, hiding a smile. It was funny

how people assumed that a doctor must know every other doctor in Australia. Australia was a mighty big country! I'm afraid I don't. I'm from Sydney,' she said. 'I've only come to Queensland for a holiday.' Emotionally bruised, battered, and in need of a rest, she thought with a hidden sigh.

'Well, never mind. Will you do it, my dear?' Zara clasped her hands together. 'Will you fill in for my ailing model? The parade will be mostly resort wear, along with some formal evening wear, and it's to be held right here by the poolside, so you can feel perfectly relaxed about it. My dear, please say you'll do it. We'll pay you, of course.'

The woman looked at her so appealingly that Gemma, who had never in her life considered stepping on to a catwalk, let alone had the slightest desire to— even if she could have found the time—nodded.

'I'll do it,' she said. 'Only, I have one condition.'

'Anything, darling. Name it.'

'Please don't tell anyone that I'm a doctor. As I said before, I'm up here on holiday—for a complete rest,' she admitted. 'I don't feel like talking about my work at all—I don't even want to think about it. If anyone asks, I'm just plain Gemma Hayes, tourist. OK?' The truth was, she couldn't face the thought of answering any questions just now. Questions about her career, her future, could lead to questions about Jonathan . . . 'It's surprising how people, once they know you're a doctor, want to discuss all their petty ailments with you,' she explained, hoping that would be sufficient to satisfy Zara, to keep her silent.

Zara chuckled. 'That's because they want advice free of charge. Lawyers have the same problem. I know, because I married one. All right, my dear, I'll keep your secret,' she promised. 'Now, about payment . . .'

'I won't take any payment,' Gemma said softly. 'Put it into the surgery fund.'

'That's good of you, dear. Dr Rivers will be most grateful, I'm sure——'

'Oh, please don't say anything to Dr Rivers. I don't want him feeling he has to thank me or anything. It's not necessary. Besides, I don't imagine I'll earn enough to make much difference.'

'You'd be surprised how much a model earns,' Zara said, her eyes twinkling. 'Almost as much as a doctor!'

Gemma smiled and shook her head. 'Not this doctor. I've been a struggling, overworked resident at a public hospital for the past two years.' And now the two years were up and she had come up here to the tropics for a well-earned rest, having put her future career 'on hold' for two healing weeks.

'You should be in private practice, Gemma, dear,' Zara said with a smile. 'Have you considered it?'

When she saw the faint cloud that flitted across Gemma's brows, she added penitently, 'Forgive me, my dear. Now *I'm* intruding,' and swiftly changed the subject. 'Meet me in my apartment in an hour's time and I'll give you a briefing. Here's where I'm staying . . .'

She plucked a pen and a printed card from her bag and scribbled something. 'We'll be having a full dress rehearsal in one of the function rooms this afternoon. You'll do just fine, dear, don't worry. You're a natural. I'd never be foolish enough to say that you've missed your calling—you've chosen a very fine vocation—but I think you could have gone far in the modelling world.'

With a sigh she floated away in a swirl of silk.

The rest of the day was more than busy enough to keep Gemma's mind off the parade in the evening, and to keep it from thinking about how nervous she was. She felt vaguely irritated that she had been denied an afternoon of windsurfing, as she had planned, but she consoled herself with the thought that it was all in a good cause. A new surgery for the resort doctor . . . She wondered fleetingly what the doctor was like. Dr Chad Rivers . . . Was he young, medium, old? She had always thought that doctors who came to work at holiday resorts were either older, semi-retired medicos who wanted a quiet, undemanding practice and a healthy, relaxed life-style, or recently qualified young doctors who wanted to gain experience and thought that a holiday resort would be a fun place to get it. And yet Zara Magatelli had spoken of Dr Rivers as though he had been at the height of his career when he came here. Why would an experienced, highly thought of doctor with a thriving practice want to waste his talents at an island resort, catering to mostly rich, spoiled holidaymakers?

He must be running away from something, Gemma decided. Maybe he'd cut off the wrong leg or made a pass at a patient. Or maybe he was just running away from the pressure of a busy city practice . . .

She dismissed Dr Chad Rivers from her mind with a feeling of mild contempt.

The evening arrived all too soon. As she and the other models gathered around Zara Magatelli for last-minute instructions, she found herself wondering what on earth she was doing there. She pictured Jonathan's tight-lipped disapproval—'You're cheapening yourself, Gemma. Parading in front of a lot of leering strangers!'

—before she remembered that it didn't matter any more whether he disapproved of what she did or not; he was no longer a part of her life.

Well, at least nobody, not even Jonathan, could complain about the *way* she looked. She had insisted on maintaining her natural look, and wore only lipstick, a dusting of powder, and a touch of eyeshadow, unlike the other girls, with their glittering eyelids and their gleaming blushers and their false mascaraed eyelashes. As for her hair, she had washed it and brushed it until it shone, and wore it hanging loose, having refused to allow the hairdresser to tease or spray it into a stiff, unnatural style that would have made *her* feel stiff and unnatural. And Zara, bless her, had backed her up. 'Gemma's hair is gorgeous the way it is—don't touch it.'

She had even managed to avoid wearing the daring one-piece swimsuit that Zara had lined up for her to wear. It was backless, high-legged and quite stunning. 'I just wouldn't feel comfortable parading in swimwear,' she protested to Zara. 'Couldn't one of the other models wear it?'

Zara hadn't given in without a fight. 'But darling, you'd look ravishing in it. Are you quite sure? You weren't a bit self-conscious this morning wandering around the pool in a bikini that was far more revealing than this swimsuit. It'll be no different tonight—you'll be parading alongside the pool, just the same.'

'It wouldn't be the same to me—parading semi-naked under bright lights with hundreds of ogling eyes looking on,' Gemma said with a wry grin. 'I'd feel more comfortable with a little more cover. Please, Zara, let the other girls wear the swimsuits—they're used to it.'

'Well, you were good enough to help me out, so have it your way. There are plenty of other outfits. You won't object to shorts, I hope? Or an occasional bare midriff?'

Gemma shook her head, and grinned, feeling that honour was satisfied.

Now that the parade was about to start, she was surprised to find herself trembling. With fear? she wondered. Or excitement? She took a quick peep outside and saw an intimidating collection of people seated at small tables around the floodlit pool beneath the swaying palms—most of the men wearing dinner-jackets, all of the women in stunning evening wear—while groups of others, dressed more casually, stood watching from the rear. Twinkling coloured lights were strung between the palms, and waiters in red coats drifted around with trays of exotic cocktails. Haunting Hawaiian music added a romantic touch to the heady, tropical atmosphere.

Once the parade started, she barely had time to think—she was swept along by the beat of the music, by the whispered instructions of the other girls, and by Zara Magatelli in the wings. She was barely conscious of the eager hands that tugged and pulled at her during each change of outfit; hardly aware even of her nervousness.

One thing she *was* conscious of—and became more so as the parade went on—was the presence of one particular man, a man she had to pass close to each time she rounded the far end of the pool. It wasn't his appearance so much that attracted her notice, although he had the craggy good looks and the long, rangy frame of a man worthy of a second glance. It was his manner, his look of utter, undisguised boredom.

Don't think I'm enjoying this any more than you are, mister, she thought sourly the first time she passed by. The second time she passed him she deliberately met his eye, steady dark brown colliding with smoky grey. There was more than boredom in his expression—she sensed contempt as well. And she would have sworn, as she let her gaze slide away, that she saw his lip curl!

If you find fashion parades so tedious, why did you bother to come? she thought with a hidden snarl of her own, while smiling serenely at the next person to fall under her gaze. She avoided his eye after that, but was uncomfortably conscious of his presence each time she swept past. Beside him, two men and an attractive dark-haired woman—his wife?—were clapping enthusiastically and smiling with obvious enjoyment. If they noticed that he wasn't sharing their pleasure, they didn't show it or seem to be affected by it.

Audible gasps greeted Gemma's final outfit, a dream of an evening dress with a white, beaded halter-bodice and a short three-tiered skirt of misty *point d'esprit* which flew out like a cloud from her slender hips, leaving her shapely knees tantalisingly exposed.

As she rounded the pool for the last time, Gemma caught the eye of the man who had struck her as suffering from terminal ennui. Now there was a different expression in his eyes: a new awareness, a gleam in the grey that looked suspiciously like admiration; only, the second he realised her eyes were on him, a shutter seemed to come down over his own, and his expression reverted to its former bored cynicism.

Maybe his wife's the jealous type, Gemma thought charitably. The type who gets jealous if he looks admiringly at another woman.

As she made her final graceful pirouette, surprised that she had managed to get through the parade without tripping and falling over, she carefully avoided looking in his direction. If the man had problems with his wife, that was his lookout. She had enough problems of her own without losing any sleep over his or anyone else's. Anyway, the man looked a crashing bore. Quite insufferable, in fact.

Zara Magatelli was delighted with the enthusiastic response her fashions had inspired, and especially pleased with her models. She thanked them all profusely, and Gemma in particular, for coming to her rescue at such late notice. Then she told them all to get dressed and go out and mingle, if they wished to, with the other guests and to 'tuck in' to the smorgasbord which lay spread out enticingly under the coconut palms. 'The food and drinks tonight, girls, are on the house.'

They went their own ways after, that, a few of the models slipping away altogether with the excuse that they needed their beauty sleep or that they were on a diet, others pairing up with bronzed young men and disappearing into the night.

Gemma made for the smorgasbord, lured by the seafood platters and the prospect of a free meal. As she tucked into the the king prawns, juggling a glass of wine in one hand and her plate of prawns in the other, a man's deep voice rumbled at her shoulder.

'Keep eating like that and you'll be out of a job.'

'Out of a job?' she echoed, turning her head in faint puzzlement—only to catch her breath as she found herself facing the man with the bored, smoky eyes.

She had to tilt her chin quite a bit to meet him eye to eye. That in itself she found vaguely aggravating. She never had to strain her neck to meet Jonathan's eyes. Jonathan's eyes were grey too, she reflected idly. Only they were a different grey. With a bit of blue in them. Or was it green? How silly. Why couldn't she remember?

'Don't models have to watch their figures?' drawled the man, his brows lifting fractionally, causing fine lines to radiate from his dark eyebrows.

She opened her mouth to retort that she wouldn't know, since she wasn't really a model at all, but his taunting manner irritated her so much that she shut it again without enlightening him. He could go on thinking she was a model, for all she cared. She had no wish to confide in the man.

Why was he bothering to talk to her, anyway, when he'd made no secret of the fact that he looked on all models with contempt? Or had that bored performance of his during the parade been merely an act for his wife's benefit? Gemma eyed him speculatively, with disdain in her eyes. Now that he was away from his wife, did he think it was safe to chat her up?

'Shouldn't you be looking after your wife?' she asked pointedly.

'My wife?'

The two words were spoken quietly, but the air between them suddenly chilled.

'That—that woman you were sitting with . . .' Gemma found herself stammering. There was a glint of ice in his eye that didn't bode well for someone. For women who pried?

' . . . Is not my wife.'

'Oh.' She bit her lip, wishing she'd kept her mouth shut. At a resort like this, you were unwise to enquire into relationships. So the woman wasn't his wife. Well, so what? Girlfriend, companion, whatever, he should still be with her, not chasing around after other women!

'Not my wife, mistress, or anything else—if that's what you're thinking.' Damn it, he could read minds! 'She came with her husband.'

'Oh,' Gemma said again, mentally chastising herself, recalling now that there had been two other men sitting at his table. She was still a bit puzzled, though. Why the sudden chill at her mention of a wife? He must *have* a wife, or why would he have reacted the way he did? Or was it she who was over-reacting? Had he given her the cold treatment simply to put her in her place and make her mind her own business?

Well, she could take the hint. She eyed him frigidly. He wasn't the only one who could dish out the cold treatment!

'My apologies, Mr . . .'

'Rivers. Chad Rivers.'

She blinked. '*Dr* Rivers?'

His mouth twisted faintly. 'I see that my fame precedes me,' he said drily. 'And just what have you heard about Dr Rivers?'

The coldness was back in his voice. Hearing it, she felt a swift flare of resentment. Who did he think he was? Somebody so important that all and sundry went around talking about him behind his back? What an insufferable ego the man must have!

She felt an overwelming urge to deflate him.

'Very little,' she said, her tone caustic. 'Zara simply mentioned that the proceeds from the parade were

going towards your surgery fund. Why, was there
something she neglected to mention?' she asked, with
something close to a sneer.

His eyes narrowed. She wasn't sure if the gleam she
caught in the icy grey was anger, a look of warning, or
the light of battle. One thing she knew, it wasn't amusement.

Then again . . . She stifled a sigh. He hid his emotions
far too well, this complex, enigmatic, aggravating man.
Did he hide his secrets as successfully? she wondered,
recalling her speculation that the resort doctor must be
running away from something.

'If we're going to continue sparring with each other,'
he said mildly, ignoring her question, 'might I know
your name?'

'Gemma Hayes. And I assure you I have no wish to
go on sparring with you. If you'll excuse me . . .'

He caught her arm as she started to move away.
Pausing, she looked coldly down at his hand, idly
noting its shape, its texture, and conscious of the
strength of his fingers, the warmth of his hand on her
bare skin. Strange to think that it was a doctor's caring
hand . . .

Not so caring now. 'You're hurting my arm.'

'I'm sorry.' He relaxed his grip. 'Pray don't let me
chase you away from your prawns. I'd never forgive
myself.' Mockery glinted in his eyes. 'Let me refill your
plate.'

She was tempted to flounce off with her nose in the
air, but the prawns won. Prawns, French rolls, and
salad. Truly, this smorgasbord was a feast fit for a . . .

A model? She recalled that, as far as Dr Rivers was
concerned, that was what she was—a model—and for

the first time it struck her as amusing. The joke was on Dr Chad Rivers—and he deserved it if she played it to the full. She piled another bread roll and an extra piece of cheese on to her plate.

With amazing self-control, he refrained from commenting.

'Aren't you eating, Dr Rivers?' she asked pleasantly. 'Would you care for a piece of celery? Some carrot? A hunk of cheese, perhaps? You must eat healthily and *stay* healthy, or people will conclude that you're not a good doctor.

And that, she thought with satisfaction, is to pay you back for your snide comments earlier—for insinuating that all fashion models must half starve themselves to keep their jobs. People have some weird notions about doctors, too, you know.

There was a telling pause. Then, 'OK, I guess I deserved that,' he said wryly. 'But aren't you being just a trifle unfair? I was doing my best to make amends for any—er—less than diplomatic comments I might have made earlier. You'll notice that I didn't utter a word just now when you deliberately played the glutton.'

So he'd known that she was deliberately baiting him before. The good doctor was no fool.

'Oh, I wasn't playing the glutton,' she said airily. 'I eat like that all the time. Especially when it's on the house.' She reached for another bread roll.

'I would have thought that models were so well-paid they wouldn't have to rely on free meals,' he murmured. He spoke teasingly, but there was still an undercurrent of something else. Cynicism? Contempt?

'Models have to work hard for their money, like anyone else,' she snapped. And at once had to hide a wry smile. What would you know about fashion models, Gemma Hayes? Only what you've observed today. In fact, she had been surprised at how hard models *did* have to work—as well as how friendly and down-to-earth most of the girls were. She had imagined models to be boringly egotistical, interested only in their looks and their clothes, and in raking in easy money so that they could afford to beautify themselves further. Gemma recalled the number of times that she, with her silky blonde hair and willowy figure, had been mistaken for a model herself—especially when she had been with Jonathan, away from the hospital. And she had tended, until now—never having known any models personally —to resent the implication that she was concerned with her looks and nothing else. But now she realised that modelling was a job like any other, as hard in many ways as her own. To do well in modelling, just as in any other profession, you had to work at it.

'Um . . . won't your companions be missing you?' She was beginning to wonder why this man who disliked models so much still wanted her company.

'Not at all,' he said, reaching for a clean plate and piling it with prawns. 'I'm over twenty-one and a free agent.'

You're over twenty-one . . . granted, Gemma retorted silently. In fact, you're over *thirty*-one. Mid-thirties, at a guess. But I'm not so sure about you being a free agent. And I certainly don't intend to risk the cold treatment again by asking—even if I cared, which I don't. It's not as if I'm ever likely to see you again . And just as well, too. It's obvious we're never going to get on.

'Ah . . .' A woman's lilting voice cut the air between them. 'I see you two have met already. Wonderful!'

CHAPTER TWO

GEMMA swung round, her heart spinning into a nose-dive when she saw Zara Magatelli's smiling face. Zara was the only one who knew she was a doctor. What exactly had she meant by, 'I see you two have met already'? Zara couldn't have told Dr Rivers the truth already, could she, despite her promise? Had the man been quietly chuckling away to himself all evening, knowing all along that she was a doctor and deliberately baiting her, deliberately playing along with her, wondering how long she would keep up her masquerade as a model?

Unseen by Dr Rivers, she met Zara's eyes and raised her eyebrow enquiringly. The woman gave an imperceptible shake of her head, and Gemma felt a flicker of relief. And gratitude. Her secret was still safe!

'I was just coming to see you out, Doctor, for that very purpose,' Zara Magatelli declared.

'Oh?' His face was as impassive as his tone.

Gemma held her breath. Please, Zara, don't tell him *now*, her eyes pleaded.

'Yes. I wanted to ask you to do a favour for me, Doctor.'

'I'll try,' the doctor promised, though his tone was wary, and discouragingly cool.

Zara was unabashed. 'Unlike my other models, who are flying out in the morning, Gemma is staying on here for a while. She's taking a well-earned holiday. Could I ask you to keep an eye on her? I'm sure you'll both find you have a lot in common,' she added mischievously.

You devil, Gemma thought, inwardly fuming. You kept my secret, but you're trying to throw us together, in the hope that I'll tell him myself.

'Unfortunately, Zara, Dr Rivers is not on holiday as I am,' she pointed out evenly. 'And I'm perfectly capable of looking after myself.'

'Of course you are, my dear. But you *are* alone, aren't you?'

'Yes, but——'

'Then it's always comforting to know there's someone around if you need—well, if you need anything,' Zara said, with an airy flick of her bangled wrist. 'Don't you agree, Doctor?'

'Oh, indubitably,' he said, and his tone enraged Gemma further. He was agreeing with Zara to get her off his back; he didn't mean a word of it. He had no intention of 'keeping an eye on her'. And she didn't want it any more than he did!

'Thank you, Doctor. I knew I could rely on you. Doctors can always be relied on . . . can't they?' said Zara ingenuously, and floated away before Gemma, gulping, could explode.

'I really must go, too,' she gasped, hoping Dr Rivers would put her discomposure down to embarrassment at Zara's suggestion, and not seek the real reason. She hid a quick smile. Truly, anyone would think she was a bank robber or an axe murderer, the way she was so bent on keeping her real profession a secret! But why should she change her mind and open up now? She had vowed when she first came here that she would forget she was a doctor for these two weeks, and not even think about her career, or, in fact, about anything back home until she felt a bit stronger, and she wasn't going to change her mind now—even to share her secret with the resort doctor. Which wouldn't make much sense now anyway, since she was leaving right this minute and she had no intention of ever seeing Dr Rivers again. Despite Zara Magatelli. And she knew that Dr Chad Rivers would share the sentiment.

'You're not going to miss out on that delectable tropical fruit salad, are you?' the doctor asked gently, making no attempt this time. Gemma noticed, to seize her arm. But she paused just the same. He had a point. It looked delicious. What was more, like the seafood and salads, it was free. Meals on the island were expensive—she'd be mad not to eat while she had the chance. Tomorrow she'd be plain old Cinderella again, the impoverished tourist—no longer the pampered fashion model. Surely she could put up with Dr Chad Rivers for a few more minutes? Assuming he meant to stay with her, of course. With a bit of luck, he would leave her to her fruit salad and go back to his friends.

When he made no move to do that, merely stepping aside for a moment to fill two bowls with juicy slices of mango, paw-paw and pineapple before drawing her away to a quieter spot behind a clump of palm trees, she couldn't resist a comment.

'You don't have to stay with me because of Zara Magatelli,' she said lightly. 'There's no need. I'm a big girl now. Like you, I'm over twenty-one and a free agent.'

Suddenly she felt a warmth along her cheeks. It was only just hitting home that she was indeed free, and it felt a bit strange. Jonathan seemed to have been around forever . . . He still might have been around, she mused, half pensive, half defiant, if he had been more reasonable, more understanding. Who would have thought he would start making impossible demands on her, practically from the moment she accepted his engagement ring? It had come as a nasty jolt, after believing for so long that he supported her medical career. Offers of partnerships in prestigious medical clinics didn't come up every day. To her, it had seemed the chance of a lifetime . . .

What it actually boiled down to was that Jonathan hadn't wanted a full-time doctor for a wife. 'I'm not asking you to give up medicine altogether,' he had argued, trying his best to be fair and reasonable. 'You could do locum work, Gemmy. Then you'd be more flexible.' But locum work had never held any appeal for her. There was no continuity in locum work . . . you couldn't get to know your patients, you couldn't build up their trust over a period of time. You were just a fill-in, a stop-gap. Jonathan had said that if she truly loved him she would be prepared to compromise. But she hadn't been prepared to. They had had fierce arguments, each accusing the other of being unreasonable. Until in the end she had given him back his ring.

'You've gone very quiet. I can see your mind ticking over.' Dr Rivers' low voice intruded on her thoughts. 'Is it something you feel like sharing?'

He was using the gentle, persuasive tones of the doctor he was, and for a moment she was tempted to confide in him. As a doctor, he more than anyone should understand her needs, her dilemma. Jonathan, being a businessman, not a doctor, could only see the

situation from his own narrow, selfish viewpoint. He
wanted a wife who was going to be around whenever he
flicked his fingers: a dutiful little housewife, a good-
looking hostess to impress his business colleagues, a
full-time mother to raise the children he wanted. *She*
wanted children too—eventually—but she wanted to
keep on practising medicine as well. She didn't see why
she couldn't successfully combine the two—plenty of
women did. But Jonathan had insisted that it wouldn't
work. Her career, her commitment to medicine, meant
nothing to him—except maybe from a prestige point of
view. She had noticed that he was always ready enough
to boast to his friends that his 'beautiful fiancée' was a
qualified doctor.

Now who's being unfair? she chided herself.
Jonathan accused you of not considering *his* life, his
feelings . . .

Could he have been right? She felt too emotionally
drained just now even to think about who might be right
and who might be wrong. Which was why she had come
here, to the serene Whitsunday Islands, to bury herself
in the sun, far away from family pressures, questions,
recriminations . . . and especially, far away from
Jonathan.

In a way, it felt strange not having him around.
They'd been friends for a long time, and he had always
been pleasant company—at least he had been until she
had agreed—rather rashly, it seemed now—to marry
him, and they had started arguing about her career. But
if there was a void now in her life, she didn't regret the
decision she had made. She was sad about it, but he'd
given her no choice. She was a doctor, and Jonathan
had known that from the beginning. It was unfair of

him to start making selfish, unreasonable demands.

She looked up into Dr Rivers' lean, craggily handsome face. It was partially in shadow, with the glow of the coloured lights playing rather eerily among the shadows. A trick of light made his eyes glint suddenly, and she felt a warning tingle at the nape of her neck. She'd be a fool to share her secrets with this man, let alone look to him for guidance. What did she know about him? How could she rely on him to give her an unbiased opinion? He had problems with his own love-life, she suspected, and a cynical outlook on life—and towards people—that she could well do without. She'd be crazy to depend on any advice from him.

'I'm just wondering why you're wasting your time with someone you don't even particularly like,' she said with a shrug.

His brow rose. 'What makes you think that?'

'Well, you've made it plain you don't think much of models.' His cynical attitude to the profession and his sweeping assumptions about *her*, simply because in his eyes she was one too, made her feel even less inclined now to confide in the man. 'And you were clearly bored to death by the fashion show,' she pressed on. 'And since we've been talking, we've hardly agreed on anything.'

'Perhaps I was drawn to you out of curiosity,' he said, his expression bland, unreadable.

'Curiosity?' Now, what did he mean by that?

'Somehow you don't seem to fit the mould.'

Her stomach gave a tiny flutter. Her face, though, was all innocence as she looked up at him. 'What mould is that?' she asked, suppressing a flare of amusement.

'The fashion model mould.'

'You're an expert on models, are you?' She regarded him challengingly. 'From close personal experience, I dare say?'

There was an imperceptible tightening of his lips. 'You could say that.'

And the experience has disillusioned you, she thought, wondering if he was thinking about one model in particular, or had had intimate encounters with several. Whichever it was, he had obviously been soured against all models as a result.

'I'm sure there are plenty of models who don't fit the general stereotype,' she said, lifting her chin.

'Not in my experience.'

There it was again. In *his* experience. Was he married to a model? Or had he been, once? Had his wife's career as a model come between them?

I know all about careers coming between true love, she thought ruefully. Aloud, she said with a hint of sarcasm, 'Well, I'm glad you're such an expert. And what makes you think I don't fit the mould? Simply because I like to eat?'

'Not only that. I noticed during the parade . . .' He paused, looking down at her with narrowed eyes, so that any expression in them was hidden. 'I noticed that you didn't parade in swimwear like the others.'

She met his look unblinkingly. 'I have this simply repulsive tattoo across my stomach,' she said.

'How unpleasant for you.' He didn't believe her; she hadn't expected him to. But he didn't pursue the subject either. 'And there was something about you,' he added musingly. 'You looked more natural than the others. Your face, your hair. You really *are* a professional model, I take it?'

Her heart jumped. She was tempted to come clean there and then, but some mischievous, stubborn impulse held her back. He was so prejudiced, so cynical, so disdainful of the whole modelling fraternity . . . so much so that he couldn't believe that one of their number might be other than deserving of contempt. If she told him she was a doctor, she knew that he would immediately look on her with new and approving eyes. Which would be taking the easy way out. Something inside her rebelled at the thought. She felt like teaching him a lesson . . . teaching him that it was more important to respect and like people for themselves, and not to be influenced by whatever career path they had chosen to follow.

'You really can't bear it, can you?' She feigned exasperation. 'You can't bear to think that your pre-conceived notions about models might be wrong. I assure you . . . ' she took a deep sip of her wine, 'there are plenty of models who don't pile the make-up on and who wouldn't dream of baring their bodies.'

At least, I assume there are, she thought, chuckling inwardly at her blithe assumptions. Gemma Hayes, the champion of the modelling fraternity! Zara would be proud of her. Or would the woman be surprised that she hadn't confided in Dr Rivers by now?

When he made no comment, she resumed her attack. 'You have a cynical view of all models because of your own experience with a few. Or was it only one?' she demanded boldly.

His eyes glittered, reflecting the cold blue thrown by one of the coloured lights dangling from the palm tree above. 'That is something that needn't concern you.' His tone held the same chill as his eyes.

'Sorry . . . Doctor,' she said, with exaggerated sweet-
ness. Keep your little secrets, she thought with a shrug.
And I'll keep mine.

His attitude made her more determined than ever not
to tell him the truth. Dr Chad Rivers had a huge great
chip on his shoulder—a one-eyed, jaundiced view of all
fashion models—and to tell him now that she was really
a doctor, not a model after all, would only reinforce his
view and give him the satisfaction of reminding her that
he had seen all along that she didn't fit the mould.
Though why it should bother her in the slightest whether
the man had hang-ups about anything under the sun, let
alone models, she couldn't imagine. It wasn't as if she
had an intimate knowledge of models herself, or had
any reason in the world to champion their cause. It was
most unlikely that she would even see him again after
tonight. She couldn't see Dr Chad Rivers bowing to a
request made by Zara Magatelli. A request from a
fashion designer.

'Want some more?' he asked, indicating her empty
plate. When she shook her head, he took it from her and
handed both plates to a passing waitress. 'Another
drink?' He reached for her glass.

'No, thank you. It's time I was——'

'Catching up on your beauty sleep?' he finished
smoothly.

'How chauvinistic. You disappoint me, Doctor.'

'Chad, please. You don't mind if I call you Gemma?'
He obviously wasn't going to lose any sleep over dis-
appointing her!

'It's hardly worth getting on to first-name terms when
we're both about to go our own ways.' She wanted him
to know that she didn't expect to see him again, any

more than he would want or expect to see her.

'Well, just in case our paths should accidentally cross,' he said, a spark of humour kindling in his grey eyes. 'Where are you staying?' he asked.

'In one of the bures, up on the hill. It's half hidden by she-oaks and bougainvillaea bushes. It's lovely.'

'I'll walk you back,' he offered.

She hid her surprise. 'Thanks, but I can find my own way.'

'I was actually looking for an excuse to leave, too. If you abandon me now I could be collared by some gimlet-eyed matron determined to regale me with her ailments.'

So he had that problem too. She sympathised. But——

'I'm sure you can cope,' she said glibly. 'You only have to tell her to make an appointment.'

He looked down at her for a moment, his eyelids flickering. 'Thanks for the tip,' he said, a whimsical note in his voice.

'I doubt if you need any tips from me, Doctor——'

'Chad.'

'Chad.' The name came surprisingly easily to her lips. It seemed to suit him, somehow. A masculine name, strong, no frills, and yet with something inscrutable about it. 'You would only have to give the poor woman one of your looks——' She stopped, biting her tongue, which the wine seemed to have loosened.

'One of my looks?' She caught a glimmer of humour in his eyes. She had half expected to see one of his 'looks' right there and then: the cold treatment he used to such devastating effect.

'I think you know what I mean,' she said lightly, and

backed away with a shrug. 'Well, come on, let's go. I'd
hate to leave you in the clutches of some complaint-
ridden matron.'

Again something flickered in his eyes. 'Thoughtful of
you. It's rare to find someone who understands what we
poor doctors have to go through.' He offered her his
arm as they turned to go, but she pretended not to
notice the gesture and fell into step beside him with her
hands clasped loosely in front of her.

'I'm afraid it's an occupational hazard . . . these
people seeking free consultations,' Chad confided
ruefully as they left the dancing lights behind. Don't I
know it? Gemma thought, hiding a smile. 'I guess in
your case,' Chad hazarded, 'you have ambitious
females bowling up to you asking you to find them
modelling assignments?'

She gave a rather choking laugh in lieu of an answer,
and vaguely spread her hands. What answer could she
give, short of admitting that she wasn't a model at all
and so had never been approached by ambitious
females? And she wasn't prepared to make any such
admission—not yet. She was beginning to enjoy her
little masquerade. After all, it wasn't hurting
anybody—least of all him. She hadn't even told any
outright lies; she had merely gone along with
assumptions—and spoken up in defence of models. All
for no better reason than that he was so clearly
prejudiced against them!

It was a pleasant stroll to the row of Polynesian bures
on the hillside, each one nestling in its own tiny piece of
bushland. The sky this evening was like star-studded
black velvet, and the air was humid and still, heavy with
exotic scents.

'You came to the island on your own?' Chad asked, breaking a short silence which had fallen comfortably between them. It was easy to feel comfortable on such a balmy, beautiful evening, and in such surroundings. A tropical paradise!

She nodded. 'It's my first real holiday in years. I just wanted to relax.' To relax and forget . . .

'I didn't realise modelling was so exhausting,' Chad said with a touch of his former derision. He held up his hand as she opened her lips to fire back a retort. 'I know, I know. Models are as hard-working as anyone else. I'm sure it's a very demanding life. All that parading around, forever dressing and undressing, always having to look good . . . To say nothing of all that formidable jet-setting from place to place . . .'

She had to stifle a giggle, because she found herself agreeing with him. It sounded positively daunting. Why did they do it? For the money? The travel? The clothes? Because they liked mixing in high society? Or liked being looked at and admired?

'Don't talk about it,' she begged, her defence suddenly crumbling. 'I'm on holiday.'

They had reached the steps of her bure. 'And what are some of the things you like to do while you're holidaying on a tropic isle?' Chad asked, appearing in no hurry to go. 'Lounge around the pool? Sunbathe on the beach? Take a leisurely cruise in a glass-bottomed boat?'

'I really prefer to be more active,' she admitted. 'I like windsurfing, water-skiing, snorkelling, sailing . . . I just love all water sports. Swimming too, of course.'

'Is that so?' He looked surprised. Remembering the delusion he was under, she felt a flare of amusement, thinking: He's surprised that a *model* would risk ruining her precious skin and messing up her hair and her nail polish doing anything so active!

She looked up at him innocently. 'You sound surprised. Don't *you* like those things? I suppose, being a doctor, you have to maintain a certain dignity. Or are you afraid you'll get hurt? The doctor needing medical treatment . . . mm, that would be bad for your image! You wouldn't be much use to your patients, either, if you were laid up.'

'I fear you're ribbing me,' he said, his lips quirking faintly. 'If you're not, then you're suffering from a few misconceptions of your own. I like to indulge in all water sports—just like you. When I'm lucky enough to have the time.'

'I thought resort doctors had it easy,' she said, in teasing retaliation for his attacks on models. Was she secretly hoping that he *would* have some spare time? And that he would want to spend it with her? It would be rather fun to have someone to talk to now and then, and do things with. It wasn't that she hadn't had other approaches—eager males predominating—but none had sparked her interest enough to encourage them. She had convinced herself that she wanted to be alone, that she *needed* to be alone, and until this evening she had stuck to that. Now she wasn't so sure . . . It might be nice to have company occasionally. And with Dr Chad Rivers, who didn't get much time off, that was all it would be—occasionally. There would be no risk of getting involved—something neither of them would want anyway.

You're getting ahead of yourself, Gemma, dear. He hasn't even suggested seeing you again!

'The actual surgery hours are reasonably civilised,'

Chad drawed, 'but I'm also on call twenty-four hours a day, and this is a big resort—the biggest and most popular along the entire Great Barrier Reef. There's a permanent staff of several hundred, and there can be over a thousand visitors here at any one time. And occasionally I get patients from the other islands as well, where they only have a nurse on duty.'

Gemma nodded thoughtfully. Perhaps he *was* kept busy, but nobody could call it a high-powered, pressurised practice. She still wondered why he was here, a doctor who presumably had been at the height of his career . . .

'Where do *you* live?' she asked him curiously. 'Here at the resort? Is your surgery also your home?'

'Heavens, no.' He shook his head. 'My surgery's only a small place. Hardly big enough for my patients. Hence the plans for a new surgery. No, I live well away from the resort . . . in fact, I live well away from everyone. Most of the resort staff live in apartments on the hill behind the harbour, but I've rented a cottage around the coast a bit, which used to belong to the owner of the island, before he built his new mansion at the far end of the island. My place isn't far from here, actually, though it feels pleasantly remote when you're there. It's secluded and peaceful. I like it.'

'And you live there alone?' She realised as she asked the question that she was stepping on to thin ice, risking the cold treatment again. But it was a natural enough question, surely?

'Yes, I live there alone.' He spoke quietly, impassively, with, she was thankful to hear, no hint of his former coldness—with no hint of any emotion at all. She wondered if he was making a conscious effort to mask his feelings from her. 'Not that I'm there all that much,' he added, his tone wry now. 'Not in the day time, at least. I'm either at my surgery, making calls, or I'm out on the water.'

'Do you have your own boat?' she asked. It sounded a rather pleasant life-style. Lonely, but pleasant.

'I do. Maybe you'd like to come for a sail some time?'

'That's very kind of you.' To her own surprise she felt a strange little flip of pleasure. 'But please don't let me keep you any longer now. I guess you're working in the morning?'

'Only until midday. It's Saturday. On Sunday I'm off all day, though I'm still on call for emergencies. I'm taking the boat out tomorrow after surgery, as a matter of fact. Be waiting for me by the pool after lunch if you'd like to come for a sail.'

It was an offhand sort of invitation. Did he think she might have changed her mind by midday tomorrow? Was he already regretting his impulsive invitation, and hoping she would? He was not an easy man to read, Dr Chad Rivers, Gemma reflected idly, as she bid him goodnight. She wasn't even sure that she'd be wise to try.

CHAPTER THREE

AFTER making herself a sandwich for lunch and washing it down with fresh orange juice, Gemma made her way to the pool. She had spent the morning windsurfing on the shallow offshore waters, and now decided to have a quiet read while she was waiting for Chad. She wondered if he would show up, or if he'd had a change of heart since last night and no longer wanted to take her sailing. He could always say later, if their paths happened to cross, that he'd been held up by a patient. As a doctor herself, she was familiar with that ploy.

She stretched out on one of the banana-yellow lounge chairs by the pool, pulling her hat down low over her eyes, since it was very bright out here in the sun, even with sunglasses, and opened her book, a paperback romance that she had picked up earlier. She knew it would be light and easy to read—a pleasant change from the heavy medical tomes and scientific journals she was accustomed to poring over. In minutes she had drifted off into pleasant unreality.

'It must be a good book.'

With a start she glanced up. 'Chad! How long have you been standing there?' Squinting against the sun, she had an impression of rippling muscles and tanned arms, and legs as brown and firm as tree-trunks.

'Long enough to wonder if you're going to want to leave that book of yours to come sailing.'

She put it down at once, swinging her legs over the side of the lounger. 'I'm sorry,' she said as she sprang to her feet. 'Of course I'm ready . . . I was just filling in time.'

'What are you reading?' he asked curiously. 'It must be gripping. I said hello three times.'

She looked at him sceptically. Had he? Dr Chad Rivers didn't strike her as the type who would stand patiently around saying hello three times to someone he barely knew. And only barely approved of!

'It's a romantic novel,' she said with a shrug. 'I wouldn't say it's terribly gripping. A light, pleasant read, that's all.'

He glanced more closely at the book in her hand, a faint sneer on his lips. 'You don't read those, do you?'

His expression seemed to be saying, Oh well, I guess that's par for the course, all fashion models being brainless twits.

She lifted her chin. 'Don't you ever read thrillers? Murder mysteries?'

'Sometimes. Why?'

'You read them for light relaxation, don't you? Well, that's why I read these. Except that there's no violence in mine . . .' She tapped the book in her hand. 'And any sex is based on love and romance—it's not just sex for its own sake. So what makes you think your thrillers are more worthy than my romances?'

He thrust out his lip. 'But they're rubbish.' He wasn't defeated yet. 'They're not even well-written.'

'Have you ever read one?'

'Never.' He gave a smug half-smile.

Got you, she thought. 'Then I suggeset you do before you start criticising them,' she said sweetly. 'A lot of them are as well-written as well as any of your thrillers. They might deal, by and large, with unreal situations, but nobody can say they're harmful. Can you say the same about your thrillers? I detest gratuitous violence in fiction.'

He looked at her thoughtfully, his eyes hidden by his dark glasses. 'You could have a point,' he conceded. Whether he agreed with her, or simply wanted to change the subject, she couldn't be sure.

'Anyway, they're written for women, not for men.' She decided to have the last word. 'So I guess any value they might have would be lost on you, Dr Rivers.'

'Quite likely.' He waved in the direction of the harbour, apparently content to let her have the last word. 'Shall we go?'

He looked younger and more relaxed today, Gemma thought, covertly examining him as they turned to go. Perhaps it was his casual attire: the cool open-necked shirt, the white shorts, the sunglasses. Again she was struck by the deep tan of his arms and legs, as though he often exposed them to the sun.

She caught the look he gave her in return, and hoped he approved of her blue and white striped top and white trousers. A sense of unaccustomed shyness—or was it self-preservation—had prompted her to abandon the brief shorts she had planned to wear in favour of ankle-length trousers. She wasn't sure enough yet of Dr Chad Rivers' motives in seeking her company today. How did she know the invitation wasn't just a novel way of saying 'Come and see my etchings'?

Knowing his opinion of models—and in his eyes, that was all she was—she wouldn't be surprised if he had an equally low opinion of their morals!

Well, Dr Rivers, she thought, making a grab at her hat as a warm gust of wind tried to to whip it from her head, if that's what you have in mind, forget it. I'm not here to get entangled with any man, let alone a man with a chip on his shoulder. Just because you happened to catch me reading a romantic novel, it doesn't mean I'm on the lookout for a holiday romance—if you could call what you have in mind a 'romance'.

By this time she had convinced herself that his intentions were anything but honourable!

'You're looking awfully grim,' Chad said, and she glanced up at him quickly, cross with herself for showing her feelings so plainly. There was amusement in the quirk of his lips, and she was sure that behind his dark glasses his eyes were laughing at her.

'It's just that my hat won't stay on.' She yanked it from her head in mock disgust. 'I seldom wear hats—I hate them.'

An eyebrow appeared above the rim of his sunglasses. 'Aren't you worried about what the sun might do to that lovely complexion of yours?'

She lifted her chin. It wasn't a compliment—there was too much heavy mockery in his tone. Mockery, and a touch of cynicism. 'If I were worried about my complexion,' she retorted, 'I would never have agreed to go sailing. I'd keep right out of the wind *and* the sun.'

'I guess that's true enough. And you're not worried about your hair, either?' He raised his hand, and lightly brushed it over her smooth, silvery-blonde hair, and she was astonished at her reaction to his touch, at the odd sensation that rippled through her. It wasn't repulsion. She didn't find his touch abhorrent. But it could hardly be pleasure either; she wanted only to recoil from the contact.

She drew away with a careless, 'Should I be? Are you expecting my hair to drop out or something, now that I've removed my hat?'

His hand had already fallen to his side. She realised then how stupid she had been to let that fleeting brush of his hand affect her, even slightly. There had been nothing suggestive, nothing particularly provocative about it. The gesture had been condescending . . . faintly disparaging, if anything. She should have ignored it, shown that she was indifferent.

She stifled a sigh. It's Jonathan, she thought, anxious to find a logical reason for her strange behaviour. I'm a bit jumpy at the moment because I've just broken off my engagement to Jonathan. An enagement made in heaven, everybody had called it . . .

She recalled how happy their parents had been, and how their friends and workmates had nodded knowingly when they had finally announced that they planned to marry. She had known Jonathan, had been going out with him, on and off, for years. Her family had been friendly with Jonathan's family for as long as she could remember. All through the long years she was labouring over her medical degree, Jonathan had been there whenever she needed an escort, or a friend to talk to.

Occasionally she had gone out with other young men, but they had quickly fallen by the wayside, usually because of her own lack of interest or her absorption in her medical studies. Jonathan had always been there, like a rock, or a comfortable cushion, perhaps, to fall on. When, half-way through her second year as a resident doctor, he had presented her with an exquisite diamond engagement ring, it had seemed right and natural to accept it. After all, they loved each other . . . they always had. Their fond parents went further, saying they were 'made for each other'.

It was only when she and Jonathan were seriously

planning their wedding and their future life together that
they had come crashing down to earth, to cold reality. She
had never expected her medical career to come between
them. Jonathan had always been so supportive in the past.
It made her wonder now just how seriously he had taken it
all along.

'Most women, when they come up here, seem to worry
about what our harsh climate will do to their hair and their
skin and their faces . . .' Chad was eyeing her speculatively
through his dark glasses, as if he couldn't quite make her
out.

'Yes, well, I haven't come up here to worry about anything,' Gemma heard herself snapping back. 'I'm here to
relax and enjoy myself . . .' As she formed the words
'enjoy myself' she could have bitten her tongue out. It
sounded as if she were saying, I'm on the lookout for a
man who can give me a good time! Would he take that as
an open invitation? To make sure he didn't, she added
hastily, 'I want to spend as much time on the water as I
can . . . Tomorrow I'm planning to do some
scuba-diving.' She didn't look at him to see if he was
disappointed. Or relieved. She chatted on about her plans
for tomorrow. 'There's a boat going out to the Reef
tomorrow, with a scuba-diving instructor and equipment
on board . . .'

'Do you have a stinger suit?' Chad asked.

'A stinger suit?' She looked at him then, and was
surprised to see that his face showed concern. *Concern*?

'Yes, you must have seen them around. They're a type
of wetsuit, to protect you against stings and bites. They're
made of lycra and they come in a variety of colours.'

'I think I have seen them, yes. But wouldn't they be
awfully hot to wear in this climate?'

'Uncomfortable or not, I consider them essential in these tropical waters. At this time of year, at least, summer being the stinger season.' Something in his tone made her glance up at him again. There was a tightness about his mouth that showed he was perfectly serious. Being a doctor, she guessed he must have seen a few serious sting cases in his time here. She, like most visitors to the Great Barrier Reef, was aware that venomous creatures existed in these warm tropical waters, but she had barely given them a thought. The beauty of the reef and the island far outweighed the dangers, as far as she was concerned. Or they had, until now.

'If you say so, Doctor,' she said meekly. 'Would I be able to hire a suit?'

'I'll get Melanie to lend you one,' Chad said. 'You're about the same size.'

She looked up at him enquiringly, conscious of a tiny, unaccountable pang. Who was Melanie? His wife?

'Melanie is my nurse-receptionist,' Chad explained, as if reading her mind. 'She and her husband Nick—Nick Dane, the resort's sales and marketing director—are coming sailing with us. Along with a business colleague of Nick's from Melbourne, a fellow by the name of Peter Moss.'

He spoke with a slight inflection in his voice that seemed to say, See? You have nothing to fear from me. Were you thinking we'd be alone? How naïve of you. You'll be one of the crowd.

'I'll look forward to meeting them,' Gemma said smoothly, wondering why it hadn't occurred to her that there might be others present. She should have seen that it was only logical. This was a small island community, and Dr Chad Rivers, the island's highly respected doctor—

assuming Zara Magatelli could be believed—would hardly want to risk his reputation by going sailing alone with one of the female guests!

Which suited her just fine. She had no wish to start any tongues wagging. She felt a vague sense of relief too that now she didn't have to go on worrying about whether Chad was a rake or not. A rake would hardly have invited other guests!

Yes, it was a distinct relief. Any slight dipping of her spirits was due simply to the fact that new people —strangers—were about to be foisted upon her. She hadn't come up here to be sociable . . . she had come here to lick her wounds, and to rest, after a hard year at the hospital. And to take a breather before irrevocably accepting the partnership she had been offered in Sydney; she didn't have to give them her answer until she went home. But she had already committed herself in her own mind, and had told Jonathan so. He had forced the decision on her by virtually giving her a choice—a full-time medical career or him. The partnership or marriage. It had been as unequivocal, as uncompromising as that.

Her parents, and Jonathan's too, she suspected with a sigh—maybe even Jonathan as well—were hoping that she would back down, have second thoughts. Even her staunchest supporter, her semi-retired doctor father, who had offered to help her financially if she accepted the partnership, had urged her, 'Be very sure, sweetheart, that you're doing what you really want.'

'It's all right—you'll like them.' Chad had noticed that she'd fallen silent and had misinterpreted it. 'Nick is a mad-keen sailor who seldom gets any time to sail these days, and Melanie is always good fun. Their Melbourne guest, Peter Moss, is suave, charming, and . . .' he paused, 'single.'

He gave her a sideways glance, which brought her chin up rebelliously. Did he think she was desperate for a man or something? Or, even more maddening, was he telling her that Peter Moss was charming and available to stop her getting any ideas about *him*? Oh, boy, Dr Rivers, Gemma fumed, have you got a lot to learn about women! Especially *this* woman!

'Well, that won't do him any good—not with me,' she said spiritedly. 'I'm not looking for a man, thanks. I came up here to get away from one!'

Damn! That had just slipped out. She jutted out her chin a bit further, to discourage him from asking any questions. If she started talking about her break-up with Jonathan, it could lead to her having to admit that she was a doctor, and that she wasn't ready to do just yet. Dr Chad Rivers needed to be taught a few sharp lessons first about jumping to conclusions about people—simply because they'd followed a career path that he, for purely personal reasons, looked on with contempt.

As far as she was concerned, he could go on thinking she was a fashion model forever. How dared he imply that she was on the lookout for a man?

Chad pretended to back away. 'I wasn't pushing you on to him—just letting you know a bit about him . . .' He grinned suddenly; an engaging grin, she had to admit. He had plenty of charm of his own—when he cared to use it. 'If he makes any unwelcome advances, just give me a nod and I'll race to your rescue. You'll be quite safe with me.'

'I'm glad to hear it,' she said drily. 'Since I know even less about you!'

'I told you last night . . . I'm over twenty-one and a free agent . . .'

She tilted her chin challengingly. 'By "free agent", I gather you mean you're not married?' Let him spell it out.

'I'm not married. Satisfied?' She listened for the chill in his voice, but heard only a note of mild humour.

But you were married once, she thought, squinting at him from behind her dark glasses. Or else you came close to it. You have your little skeletons, Dr Rivers, just as I have.

'Perhaps I'd be safer with Nick Dane,' she said aloud, with a quick shrug. 'You did say his wife's coming along too, didn't you?'

Chad looked down at her 'Why do I have the impression that you could look after yourself perfectly well, even in the company of Bluebeard himself?' he drawled, one dark eyebrow shooting upwards.

It's all those years studying and working in a male-dominated profession, she thought wryly, and chuckled silently because he still didn't know about any of that—and she wasn't about to tell him. If he was ever going to learn to like her, and respect her, it would be for herself, not because she had chosen to be a doctor.

'You'd better believe it,' was all she said, with the hint of a smile.

The harbour lay before them now, a sea of coloured sails and dancing reflections and intense blue water, with rows of impressive yachts and catamarans and cruise-boats lining the marina. It was a tranquil, picturesque scene that lifted Gemma's spirits at once. The sight of water always did.

Chad's yacht, when he pointed it out, nearly took her breath away.

'Wow! I wasn't expecting anything quite so grand,' she admitted. 'Chad, it's beautiful!'

'Glad you approve. Down below there's a cabin for two, a saloon, a galley, and quarter-berths in the aft section. It's quite comfortable.'

'That's an understatement. It's a magnificent boat. How many does it take to sail it?' she asked.

'It can be handled by one person, but it's easier with two and a breeze with more. When I'm on my own I can use the auto-helm, which steers the boat electronically, giving me a chance to rest or to tighten up the headsails or change the tension in the halyard, or whatever.'

She saw him wave to someone on board—and realised it was the woman who had been sitting next to him at the fashion parade last night. There was a man in a striped T-shirt standing beside her, and Gemma recognised him as one of the two men who had been with them. The other man from last night was there as well, handling ropes in the stern.

As Chad helped her aboard, the woman stepped forward to meet her.

'Melanie Dane . . . Gemma Hayes. Gemma . . .' Chad indicated the man in the striped T-shirt. 'This is Peter Moss, from Melbourne.' Gemma was sure Chad's eyes were mocking her behind his dark lenses. Peter Moss was a strikingly handsome young man, in fair-skinned, sleek-haired, smooth-faced sort of way. And yet she hadn't given him a second glance last night—she had been too uncomfortably aware of Dr Chad Rivers, exuding disapproval and boredom from his seat at the same table.

Melanie was all smiles as she welcomed Gemma aboard; in fact her red lips looked as if they never stopped smiling. It was contagious, and Gemma smiled back spontaneously. No wonder Chad had said she was 'good fun'. She was attractive too, rather square-faced, with thick,

dark hair pulled back into a long fall behind. Her eyes
were hidden behind the obligatory sunglasses. Up here,
only the foolhardy would step outside without them.

'Nick, come and meet Gemma.' Chad sounded
perfectly at ease. It was obvious he liked the
Danes.

Nick's handshake was as warm as his greeting. He gave
the impression that he would be enthusiastic about
anything he took on. He was pleasant-faced rather than
handsome, with fair hair burnished a deep gold in the
sunlight, and his smile was boyishly appealing. Gemma
noticed laughter-lines radiating beyond the rim of his dark
glasses. They're a nice couple, she thought, relaxing.

Nobody asked her any awkward personal questions,
merely commenting briefly on how much they had enjoyed
the parade, and then concentrating on the job in
hand—starting the engine, releasing the slip lines, and then
carefully manoeuvring the big yacht out of the harbour.
Once outside the narrow entrance, Nick and Melanie leapt
into action to hoist the sails, while Chad, at the wheel, cut
the engine. Gemma, seeing that her help wasn't needed,
kept out of their way.

It meant that in those early moments, she and Peter
Moss were rather thrown together, and it didn't take her
long to discover that he was as shallow and as smooth-
tongued as he was good-looking. His fatuous compliments
and frank admiration only succeeded in irritating her.
Even the breathtaking beauty of the Whitsunday Passage,
with its misty islands and its wide expanse of glorious
turquoise water, failed to divert him. In desperation, she
encouraged him to talk about his work. She learned that
he worked at a Melbourne travel agency, and had flown
up here to see the island resort at first hand.

'Unfortunately, though——' as he uttered the words, his long-lashed eyes slid down her body, drawing a shiver of repugnance from her '—I have to fly home tomorrow.'

'What a pity,' Gemma murmured, backing away as he shifted closer. She threw an imploring look in Chad's direction, dimly hoping he might honour his promise to rescue her, and was surprised when he waved Nick over to take the wheel and came swinging over to where she and Peter Moss were standing near the bow of the boat.

'Peter, my dear fellow,' Chad said, so affably that Gemma began to wonder if it was pure coincidence that had brought him hastening to her side, 'you'll get sunstroke and shocking windburn if you don't protect that pale skin of yours. If you go down to my cabin, you'll find some zinc cream on the bench and a shady hat. I advise you to plaster the zinc cream on your nose and to wear the hat whenever you're out in the sun.'

'Oh . . . um . . . OK.' With a nod, Peter Moss backed away, as if deciding that Dr Rivers was not a man you stood around arguing with.

Chad winked at Gemma. 'The marines to the rescue.' He gave a mock bow.

'Thanks,' said Gemma, adding with a grimace, 'If he's your idea of suave and charming, I don't think much of your taste!'

'I thought his type might appeal to you,' Chad drawled, and she looked at him sharply—and wished that his eyes weren't hidden behind his dark glasses. Surely he couldn't be serious?

'At the parade last night,' Chad went on impassively, 'your young Romeo confessed he'd had some success with models in the past. And Melanie saw him disappear into the shrubbery later with one of them.'

Gemma pulled a face. 'And so naturally you thought I'd be ready to run off with him too!'

'Would I have swooped so readily to your rescue if I had thought that?'

'But you wouldn't have been too surprised if I'd succumbed to his irresistible charm,' Gemma persisted drily.

He didn't deny it.

'You really don't think much of me, do you?' Gemma said with an exasperated sigh.

'Not true. When you get to know me better, you'll see that I don't bother much with people I don't care about. Let alone come charging to their rescue.'

When you get to know me better . . . Gemma felt a funny little quiver run through her. Did he want to get to know her better? Did she want to get to know *him* better? You could be playing with fire here, Gemma Hayes, she warned herself. Do you honestly think you could go on seeing this man and remain indifferent to him? You need that kind of complication like a hole in the head! Think of your future . . . your career. Careers and emotional involvements don't mix. You've proved that already.

To keep the sentiment in mind, she tried to conjure up Jonathan's face. Not very successfully. Why did his image always look so fuzzy, so indistinct, lately? Was it guilt, blocking it out? Guilt that she wasn't missing him more, that she wasn't pining for the old times they'd had together?

'I'll send Melanie along to chat with you.' Chad swung away. His tone was clipped, with a coolness about it that made her wonder if he was already regretting what he had said a moment ago. Mustn't have our esteemed doctor giving a girl the wrong idea, Gemma reflected sourly. You ought to be glad you're safe, Gemma, my girl . . .

A few seconds later Melanie joined her at the rail.

'Nick's in his element when he takes over the wheel . . . he loves to sail.' Her tone was affectionate, but there was a yearning note in it that brought Gemma's eyes to her face.

'He doesn't have a boat of his own?' she asked curiously. Most people living on the island seemed to.

Melanie removed her sunglasses and pulled out a handkerchief to wipe the lenses. 'He used to have a neat eighteen-footer, but he sold it when he took on this new job. I suppose Chad'd told you he's the resort organisation's sales and markerting director? He just doesn't have time these days to go sailing—in fact, he rarely has any time off.'

In repose, her face showed lines of discontent around her mouth that weren't evident when she smiled, and there was a wistfulness shadowing her dark eyes. Most people probably wouldn't have been aware of either, but Gemma noticed these things because, as a doctor, she was used to looking for them. She had worked recently in the psychiatric unit at the hospital, where she had become deeply interested in the psychological aspects and causes of illness, an area that had been sadly lacking in her medical training. She had come to see how important it was to treat the whole patient, not merely the disease.

'Oh, don't think I'm complaining,' Melanie added hastily, as she slipped her sunglasses back on. 'I know Nick is working overtime for *us* . . . for our future. That's why he sold the boat. He wanted to invest the money and see it grow. With my salary on top of his, we're hoping to save up and buy a business of our own one day. A charter-boat business. That's our dream.' Although she was smiling again, Gemma sensed that there was something not quite right.

'Do you and Nick have a family, Melanie?' she asked gently. The couple would be in their early thirties, she guessed.

The girl's lips twisted. 'If Nick were home more, we might have some hope of starting one. He works long hours, and he's away a lot. There's no problem medically . . . we've both had the all-clear there.' She drew back suddenly. 'I don't know why I'm telling you all this. Anyone would think you were a doctor or something, rather than a beautiful young fashion model, up here on holiday.' She gave a self-conscious laugh. 'Sorry to bore you.'

'You're not boring me. My—my father's a doctor, as a matter of fact,' Gemma said impulsively. 'I guess I'm just interested in people, the way he is.'

Melanie looked at her for a long moment, her expression veiled by her blue-tinted sunglasses. 'You're a nice girl, Gemma, and I'd like to give you a word of advice. I hope you won't take it the wrong way.' She paused, biting her lip. 'Gemma, don't go getting any ideas about Chad Rivers, just because he's being kind to you. I must admit it baffles me rather, because normally he doesn't have any time for fashion models. You should have heard him on the subject before the fashion parade last night.'

'I know what Chad thinks of models. And I have no intention of getting any ideas about him.' Gemma looked across the bottle-green water at the shapes of the many islands, the silhouette of each one lying across the next; islands clothed with bush and rain forest, with glimpses now and then of sandy beaches, waving coconut palms, and tall mountain peaks. An enchanting, tranquil world. 'He's only looking after me because Zara Magatelli asked him to. Anyway,' she added recklessly, hoping it would get back to Chad, 'I already have someone back home. Someone who wants to marry me . . .' She flushed at her use of the present tense. And yet the statement wasn't altogether inaccurate. Jonathan would, she was sure, still marry her—*if* she agreed to his terms.

'Who wants to marry *you*,' Melanie echoed, eyeing her shrewdly. 'And how do you feel about him?'

'I'm . . . not sure,' Gemma admitted honestly. What *were* her feelings for Jonathan? Surely, if she still loved him she would be feeling more pain? 'He—he insists I give up my career,' she heard herself telling Melanie, 'and I'm not prepared to do that.'

'He doesn't like you being a model?'

Gemma swallowed, She was treading a slippery path here. Why hadn't she kept her big mouth shut. 'He'd like a full-time wife, who will be full-time mother to his children . . . that's what it boils down to. He doesn't mind me doing a bit of——' she nearly said 'locum work', but bit the words back in time '—part-time work, but that's it.'

'And you're not prepared to do that?' Melanie asked. There was a poigant note in her voice, and Gemma had the feeling that Melanie herself would have given up her job like a shot to become a full-time wife and mother.

She shook her head. 'No.'

'Then you can't love him,' Melanie said flatly. 'Gemma . . .' She lowered her voice, even though there was no fear of being overheard from where they were standing. 'I suspect you're vulnerable right now. Don't let Chad's bedside manner lull you into thinking he could be interested in you. Seriously, I mean.'

Gemma frowned faintly. 'I haven't noticed any bedside manner,' she said with a flare of spirit. 'And you've already warned me not to get any ideas about him. As if I would! I don't need any more men messing up my life!' At the same time, she wondered if it was genuine concern that lay behind Melanie's warning, or if there was something deeper behind it. Chad, after all, was a very attractive man, and as far as Gemma knew he was unattached. Melanie, on the other hand, was in intimate contact with him every day, and right now she was feeling lonely and neglected . . .

If anyone was vulnerable, surely it was Melanie herself? *I* certainly don't intend to get entangled with Dr Chad Rivers—or any other man, Gemma asserted silently. My career is all that matters to me. It's why I gave up the man I love . . .

She frowned again, recalling Melanie's words: 'Then you don't love him . . .' Perhaps it was true that she hadn't really loved Jonathan at all, or hadn't loved him *enough*. Would her decision have been different if her love for him had been stronger? If it had been stronger than her love for her work?

She shifted uneasily at the rail. Perhaps Melanie's warning was worth heeding, after all. If she became involved with another man—say, with a man like Chad Rivers—and lost her heart completely next time . . .

She tightened her lips. It mustn't be allowed to happen! Her work, her career, had to come first. For heaven's sake, hadn't she learnt from her engagement to Jonathan? Another emotional entanglement was the last thing she wanted—it could threaten everything she had worked for!

She heard Melanie's voice at her ear, approval enriching its pleasant tone. 'Well . . . I'm glad to hear it. Because he'd never marry you.' There was sympathy rather than malice in her voice. 'I don't believe he'll ever want to marry again, but that aside, he'd never marry a model,' Melanie spelt out. 'He once told me so.'

'Is that because he was once married to a model?' Gemma asked carelessly.

Melanie shot her a look. 'Good heavens, no! What makes you think that? His wife was an artist. A brilliant one. She painted landscapes, portraits . . . Chad must have loved her very much. He still finds it difficult to talk about her.'

'They're divorced, I take it?'

'Divorced?' Melanie's brow shot up. 'No, certainly not. He's a widower. His wife died two, two and a half years ago . . . right here on this island.'

CHAPTER FOUR

'IT WAS a terrible tragedy,' Melanie said with a sigh. 'You must have read about it at the time it happened, even if you didn't know who she was.'

Gemma looked at her enquiringly, waiting for her to go on.

'It was one of those rare, freakish tragedies—doubly tragic because we didn't have a full-time doctor on the island then—and the nurse who was here at the time was useless—she says she didn't even get the call. From what I've heard about her since, I suspect she ignored it because she was having too much of a good time. Chad is convinced that if his wife had had immediate medical treatment—resuscitation, and a shot of antivenom—she just might have been saved.'

The doctor in Gemma came to full alert. 'Antivenom?' she echoed. 'What was it for? Snakebite? Stone-fish?'

Melanie shook her head. 'She was stung in the water by a box jellyfish. One of the rare Chironex species—the deadliest box jellyfish in Australia. She died within minutes—a perfectly healthy adult. I'd met her only a few days before, and she was a beautiful girl, full of life. It was tragic.'

Gemma bit back a gasp. Chad had warned her about the dangerous 'stingers', as they were called, that abounded in these tropical waters during the summer. Little wonder. His own wife!

'How awful,' she said in a whisper, her gaze flickering round in mute sympathy. Chad was standing, relaxed yet alert, at the wheel, listening to something Nick Dane was saying, and just as she turned he threw back his head in a burst of laughter. She hadn't heard him laugh like that before. He rarely smiled, let alone laughed aloud. Somehow, it struck her as poignant, in light of what she knew now about his tragic past.

'Where was Chad when it happened?' she asked, her heart going out to him. 'Was he on the island too?'

'Sadly, no. The poor girl might have had a chance if Chad had been around. She had come over here alone, just for a few days, to paint. They were living in Mackay at the time. Chad had a thriving practice there.'

'So Chad chose to come here to work *after* the—the tragedy?' Gemma bit her lip. 'How could he bear it?

'That shows the type of man his is, doesn't it?' Melanie's voice softened. 'The type of dedicated doctor he is. He wanted to see a reliable, full-time medical service on this island, to avoid a similar tragedy happening again. At times there are over a thousand people on this island.'

'Yes . . . I see.' Gemma fell silent, immersed in her own thoughts. It certainly explained why Chad hadn't wanted to talk about his wife—especially to someone who was a virtual stranger to him. But it didn't explain everything.

She still didn't know why he had such withering contempt for fashion models. Had he had an involvement with a model since coming to work on the island? An involvement which had ended unhappily, souring him against all models? He would have had ample time—it was over two years, Melanie had said, since his wife had died.

They had no further chance to talk, because Peter Moss emerged just then from below, his handsome face shaded

by a navy and white cap which had seen better days, and
the line of his finely chiselled nose marred by a dot of
white zinc cream. He looked ruefully self-conscious, and
Gemma had to choke back a giggle. Had Chad
deliberately set out to humiliate the man? Or had he been
genuinely concerned about Peter's fair complexion? She
had her suspicions.

'How about some drinks?' Melanie suggested, heading
for the galley without waiting for an answer.

'I'll come and help you,' offered Gemma, but the girl
waved her back with a quick, 'You stay with Peter—I'll
manage.'

Was she trying to push them together? Gemma
wondered. Or . . . was she trying to keep her away from
Chad? She glanced round again, and this time she caught
Chad's eye. He gave her a wave, and as she felt Peter Moss
closing in, deliberately brushing his bare arm against hers,
she said brightly, 'Let's join the others, shall we? I'd like a
turn at the wheel, if they'll let me.'

She didn't look around to see if Peter's zinc-covered
nose was out of joint; nor did she give him a chance to
demur, leading the way without a backward glance.

Half-way there, a gust of wind caught them and she
heard an exclamation from behind. She turned to see Peter
grabbing in vain for his cap as it was whipped from his
head. She watched in some amusement as it flew over the
rail, skimmed through the air and, with a graceful glide,
landed on the rippling turquoise water.

'Darn!' Peter growled, straining over the rail in a
hopeless attempt to retrieve it.

'Hat overboard!' Gemma yelled, tossing a grin in
Chad's direction.

Chad shouted back, 'There's a boat-hook just behind

you . . . you might be able to fish it back in. I'll bring the boat round.'

'By the time the boat had turned, with Nick leaping into action to lower the sails and slow the boat, Peter had found the pole and was leaning dangerously over the rail trying to hook the cap on to the end.

'Careful!' shrieked Gemma, but her warning came too late. With a shriek and a plop, Peter followed the cap into the water. 'Chad!' her head whipped round. 'Peter's——'

Chad raised a hand to show that he had seen what had happened, and a second later she heard the engine cough to life. Nick grabbed a lifebelt and tossed it overboard, quipping over his shoulder, 'He might have told us he wanted to go for a swim!'

No one appeared unduly concerned; conditions in the Passage today were near perfect. Gemma leaned over the rail, searching the calm sapphire water with a faint smile on her lips. Poor Peter! He would never live this down.

As her eyes swept the water, uneasiness caught at her throat, her smile fading when she saw there was no sign of Peter Moss. He should have surfaced by now . . .

She recalled Chad's warning about stingers. And she knew they weren't the only dangers lurking in these waters. She had a vision of sharks, of sea snakes, of the venomous blue-ringed octopus . . .

She gave a shudder.

With relief she saw an arm emerge from the water, waving weakly; then momentarily a face appeared, only to sink beneath the surface again. She gave a shriek. 'Peter's in trouble! I'm going in!'

Without pausing to think about it, without waiting for a signal from Chad, she kicked off her sneakers, climbed over the rail, and jumped in, shirt, long trousers and all.

With steady, powerful strokes, she thrashed through the water. Peter's head appeared again, directly in front of her. He was gasping for air, his eyes wild and glassy, water streaming down his pale face. She grabbed him from behind, uttering words of comfort as she supported him.

'It's all right, Peter, I've got you.' She spied the drifting lifebelt nearby, which in his panic Peter had failed to see, and, dragging him through the water, she somehow managed to slip it over his head and shoulders.

Voices were shouting from the boat, 'Hold on, Gemma, we're coming alongside! Have you both aboard in a jiffy!'

Gemma heard a splash behind her, and jerked her head round to see Chad's face level with her own, his powerful arms reaching out to assist her, his wet hair plastered to his head, his tanned face glistening with water.

'I've got him, Gemma . . .' For a moment their eyes met, and a current of unaccustomed warmth passed from the grey depths, a warmth that she could feel her own eyes instinctively responding to. Then Chad switched his attention to the man in distress.

'He's barely conscious,' she said worriedly. 'I hope nothing's bitten him . . .' She clamped her lips shut, wishing she hadn't said that. Chad didn't need her to remind him of the possible dangers . . . and what they could lead to. Peter, though, didn't appear to be in any pain, which surely was a good sign.

'Let's get him aboard.' Chad's tone was brisk, business-like. Now there was only a doctor's concern in his eyes. 'Are you too exhausted to help me hand him up to Nick and Melanie?'

She shook her head. It took only seconds to haul Peter Moss aboard, and then Chad's strong arms, with help from Nick and Melanie from above, were dragging her out of the water and over the side. She tried to stand, with the intention of going to Peter Moss's aid, but her legs seemed to have turned to rubber and they gave way beneath her. As she tried to get up, she saw Chad heave himself aboard.

'Look after Gemma,' he rapped at Melanie, dropping to his knees beside Peter, who was coughing and spluttering and trying to sit up.

'I'm sorry,' Peter gasped. 'I—I feel such a fool. I'm a lousy swimmer and I must have panicked when I felt myself go under. I—I kept swallowing water.'

Chad's face remained commendably impassive, though Gemma, eyeing him shrewdly, was certain she saw a muscle in his cheek twitch. With relief? she wondered. Or mild scorn?

'I'd better just check you over,' Chad said, and proceeded to do so, while Gemma sat with Melanie's arm around her, assuring the worried girl that she was 'as right as rain' and that it was only her legs that were wobbly.

'You'll do,' she heard Chad say to Peter a few moments later, and there was little sympathy in his voice. Chad, she suspected, wouldn't have a whole lot of time for a man—for a travel agent, in particular—who had never bothered to learn to swim properly, and who panicked even in ther calmest of seas.

She looked at the hunched, woebegone figure sitting beside Chad on the deck, and felt sudden laughter bubbling inside her. Peter's hair was hanging in unattractive wet spikes across his brow, and the dab of white zinc cream was still evident on his nose, even after his drenching. So much for Peter Moss, the sophisticated ladies' man! I bet Chad has changed his mind about him being suave and charming after all this, she thought in amusement, and, just as she had the thought, Chad glanced round and caught her eye.

She saw him pat Peter Moss rather condescendingly on the shoulder, rise, and step over to where she was sitting.

'Now, young lady,' he said. 'Your turn'.

She looked at him in alarm. 'You're not examining me! I'm fine, thanks.' Melanie, she noted in dismay, was already rising, backing away. She felt like making a grab for her, calling her back, but she realised how pathetic that would look.

'I saw you trying to stand up before. You didn't look too fine to me.' Chad was on his knees beside her now, pushing back her wet hair and peering into her face. She swallowed, and tried to meet his calmly in the eye, but his nearness was having a strange effect on her. She was finding it hard to breathe. And suddenly, despite the fact that she was wet through and her sodden shirt and trousers were clinging to her body like a second skin, she felt stiflingly hot.

'I think I'd better move into the shade,' she said uneasily, blaming the direct sunlight for the sudden rush of heat to her face.

'I'd advise you to get out of those wet clothes,' Chad said quietly.

Her cheeks flamed, hotter than ever. 'If I'd known I was going for a swim, I'd have brought a change of clothes,' she shot back facetiously, in an attempt to cover up her fluster. 'Not to worry,' she added carelessly. 'I'll dry off in no time in this hot sun.'

'Not if you move into the shade you won't,' Chad pointed out mildly. Twisting round, he called out to Melanie. 'Mel—did I see you with a beachbag earlier? Don't suppose you'd have something Gemma could change into, would you?'

'Only a bikini. Would that do? We're about the same

size.'

'That would do fine,' said Chad, and Gemma's flushed cheeks positively scorched. If she'd worn shorts instead of trousers to begin with, they'd have been half-dry by now and she wouldn't be faced with this situation. Oh, what the hell? she thought. People up here wear bikinis all the time . . . why be coy about it? Do you think Dr Chad Rivers has never seen a semi-naked body before?

'Here, I'll help you up,' Chad offered.

'I don't need any——' she began, but as she tried to rise she tottered, almost losing her balance, and found that she was grateful for his support after all. 'Thanks,' she muttered.

He was smiling into her face, a crookedly attractive smile that brought a silvery sparkle to his grey eyes and did nothing to calm her frayed nerves. 'Gemma, my girl, you're continually surprising me,' he said admiringly. 'The way you leapt overboard just now without a moment's hesitation . . .'

She tilted her chin. 'You mean you wouldn't have been surprised if I'd stood by and let the poor man drown?'

Still smiling, he denied the charge with a shake of his head. 'Let's say I wouldn't have been surprised if you'd called out to Nick or me to jump in for you.'

'Well, I——' She felt flustered and embarrassed, and a bit indignant at the same time. When would he start thinking more highly of her? 'If Melanie had been on deck,' she added with a shrug, 'she would have done the same. Anyone would have. Anyway, you and Nick were busy sailing the boat.'

'I don't think too many people *would* have done the same,' Chad said quietly. 'Especially after all my warnings about stingers.'

Gemma bit her lip. 'Chad, I——' She was about to own up that she knew about his wife, and could understand his concern, but Melanie was moving in on them and it didn't seem the right time to mention it.

'I'll take Gemma down,' Melanie offered, slipping her arm through Gemma's. As Chad backed away, Gemma swung her head round.

'Oh, I nearly forgot.' She dug into the belt of her wet trousers and pulled out a sodden object. 'Here's Peter's hat.'

Chad's eyes gleamed with sudden humour, and something else she couldn't read. 'You're a cool one, aren't you?' He took it from her and held it aloft for the others to see. 'Saving a man's life wasn't enough for you. You had to save his hat as well!'

She dismissed his praises with an airy, 'I just happened to see it floating nearby and made a grab for it without thinking. I could see that Peter was going to be OK, and that all I had to do was support him until you brought the boat alongside.'

'Gemma, you have hidden talents,' Chad said with a shake of his head.

If only you knew, Gemma thought, nursing with mischievous satisfaction the secret she was still keeping from him. 'Don't most people?' she asked flippantly.

He ignored that. 'I have a feeling, Miss Hayes, that you could do just about anything you set your mind on doing. Why you chose to become a model I'll never know. Of course, with your looks . . .' He shrugged. 'And the money you must rake in.'

'I'm sure I don't make any more than a doctor,' she retorted, with more accuracy than he knew. She tossed back her head. 'And I never said I did modelling to the exclusion of everything else.'

'Oh?' A flicker of interest kindled in the grey eyes.

She bit her lip. It would have been so easy to tell him the truth, there and then. And it was tempting, no doubt about it. Until she thought what it would mean. Instant respect. Instant rapport. The easy way out. She would rather gain his respect the hard way. By *earning* it. And she could feel that she was beginning to, very gradually. Gemma had always taken the most difficult route. Why change now?

She shrugged non-committally, and let the chance slide away. It was only when she saw the faint sneer on Chad's lips that she suffered a qualm. But instantly she dismissed it. She would tell him when she was good and ready—not a moment sooner.

'Come on, Gemma.' Melanie plucked at her arm. 'Let's get you out of those wet things so we can spread them out to dry.'

'Yes, off you go,' said Chad, turning away. 'Nick!' he shouted. 'Let's get going!'

'Aye aye, skipper!'

Down in the cabin, as she changed into Melanie's brief hot-pink bikini—the colour was louder than she would have chosen for herself, but beggars could hardly be choosers—Gemma paused to look about her. It was a comfortable cabin, with two single bunks covered in a rough-textured fabric with an attractive sea motif. Above one of the bunks hung a painting in a narrow timber frame.

She moved over to examine it more closely. It was an oil painting of the sun setting over tranquil waters, with a group of mystical islands in the background and gold-tipped clouds above. The Whitsunday Passage . . . She noticed the name 'Rivers' at the bottom and recalled Melanie telling her that Chad's wife had been an artist.

A *renowned* artist . . .

Gemma's brows puckered. She was no expert, but she could see that, though this painting was good, evoking a true feeling for the beauty of the Whitsundays, it was not a *great* painting. Thinking it must be one of Chad's wife's earlier works, she peered more closely at the painting, looking for a date. She couldn't find one, but she noticed with a jolt that the Christian name scrawled in front of the signature 'Rivers' was not a woman's name at all, but a man's. 'Chad Rivers'!

Well . . . so Chad had hidden talents too. It seemed they both had things to discover about each other!

She gathered up her wet clothes, mounted the narrow stairs, and emerged on deck, the sun's heat on her bare skin making her all too conscious of her scanty attire. Well, so what? she thought impatiently. She couldn't stay covered up forever—not in this climate! For goodness' sake, she had never been a shrinking violet before; what was it about Dr Chad Rivers that was making her into one now?

She saw Nick standing at the wheel, with Melanie at his side. Chad and Peter Moss were hovering nearby, waiting to go down below, and she hastened past them with barely a glance, avoiding Chad's eye. As she was spreading out her shirt and slacks on deck, feeling a trifle self-conscious as she placed her bra and panties beside them, Chad popped up behind her.

'Well, that's more sensible,' he applauded as she straightened, all too aware that Melanie's hot-pink bikini revealed more than it concealed. 'I take it you did come to the tropics to soak up the sun . . . so you might as well dress for it.'

His frank scrutiny sent a wave of unaccustomed

shyness sweeping through her. Annoyed with herself, she answered more sharply than she otherwise might have. 'I dressed today to go sailing, not sunbathing. What the devil are you staring at?' she snapped, nervously aware that his gaze had settled unwaveringly on her bare midriff.

'My apologies,' he said without shifting his gaze or looking the least bit repentant. 'I was looking for your tattoo.'

'My *what*? Oh,' she said as she remembered. She had the grace to blush. 'Well, you asked for that,' she said lamely. 'Making all those assumptions about me, without even knowing me, just because you once knew a model, or still know one for all I know, who's turned you against anyone who dares to tread a catwalk.'

He glanced up, a tiny spark glowing in his eyes. She didn't wait for him to speak. 'I see you're not denying it,' she said, deciding that attack was the best form of defence. It was working, too. She didn't feel a bit self-conscious any more.

'Why should I?' he murmured. 'I see you have me all summed up.'

Her eyes narrowed. 'Accurately?' she asked, prepared to listen if he cared to explain.

'I plead guilty.' But he didn't explain—he changed the subject instead. 'Peter's taking a nap down below. He nearly went to sleep just now at the wheel, only seconds after offering to take a turn. Not wanting him to run us on to a reef, I suggested he go down and sleep it off.'

'Are you quite sure he's all right?' Gemma asked, her professional concern prompting the question. 'Do you think he might have hit his head when he fell into the water?'

'No, I don't.' Something glinted in Chad's eyes as he

misinterpreted her concern. 'I see you're not as indifferent to him as you've been making out. He's fine. Just exhausted. As you must be.' His eyes bored into hers, as moments earlier they had bored into her bare midriff. Only now they showed concern. Nothing more, she told herself as her heart gave a tiny leap.

'Couldn't be better,' she assured him, and though she spoke flippantly, she meant it. 'Fit enough,' she added with a lift of her chin, 'to swim all the way back to the island for help if anyone does shipwreck us.'

Chad's lip quirked. 'You're not content with one rescue a day? You're a remarkable woman, Gemma Hayes. But an unfair one.'

'Unfair?' she echoed, looking faintly puzzled.

'Don't you think it's my turn next time to come to the rescue, if anyone needs rescuing? What are you trying to do? Dent my male ego?'

'I guess I'm just used to fighting my own battles,' she said with a grin that only partly covered a sigh. She'd had to fight plenty of battles in her time to gain acceptance in her profession Why was it, she lamented, that willowy, good-looking blondes were seldom taken seriously? People seemed to think that she'd only chosen to study medicine to prove a point, or to fill in time until she ran off to get married. She had the impression that most of them expected her to grow tired of 'playing doctor' sooner or later and retire gracefully from the scene, leaving it to the genuinely dedicated souls.

She frowned, pursing her lips thoughtfully. For the first time, she found herself wondering if it could have been that sexist attitude, those unfair misconceptions, that had prompted her decision to keep on working full-time after she was married, despite Jonathan's entreaties to cut down on her hours and allow herself time to be a wife and a mother. Was she still trying to prove something to the world? And was she putting that need, that determination, before her own happiness?

'I think I've lost you,' Chad said quietly.

She blinked, and felt herself flushing. What a time to start thinking about Jonathan!

'Sorry,' she said, and with a bright smile changed the subject. 'I like Nick and Melanie very much,' she said warmly. 'I gather Nick leads a pretty busy life. They must be enjoying having an afternoon off together . . .'

Suddenly Chad gave an exclamation. 'Talking of having an afternoon off, I promised I'd have the other three back at the marina by five. They're having dinner with some VIPs from the mainland. We'd better start heading back. Want to come and take the wheel for a while?'

She nodded, though she couldn't help wondering if he had deliberately avoided her question about Nick and Melanie. Could that mean he had something to hide? Being Melanie's boss, he must be aware that Nick often left his wife alone at night. Had Chad ever consoled her during those long, lonely hours? Had Melanie ever consoled *him*? Chad was on his own a lot too . . . and Melanie, whom Chad had described as 'good fun', struck Gemma as a very sympathetic woman . . .

CHAPTER FIVE

CHAD eased the boat in, edging up to the wharf with the gentlest of bumps. Nick deftly tossed a rope over a mooring pile and secured it with a flick of his wrist, while Melanie ran aft to do the same thing at the stern.

Gemma had changed back into her own clothes, which had dried quickly on the sun-drenched deck. She was standing with Peter Moss, who had emerged from below a few moments earlier, looking rumpled, wan and sorry for himself.

'Thanks for jumping in after me,' he said in an abashed tone, avoiding Gemma's eye.

'All in a day's work,' Gemma said lightly. She had a feeling she wouldn't be seeing or hearing from Peter Moss again. He was the type who wouldn't relish being indebted to a woman; he would picture himself in the hero's role. His self-image, she sensed with some amusement, had been severely dented by this afternoon's misadventure.

And what about Chad? she found herself wondering. Would *he* want to see her again? She tried to tell herself that she wouldn't care if he didn't, but she knew in her heart that it wasn't true. Despite her doubts about him, despite the shadows that she sensed lay behind his cynical, often unreasonable attitude, and despite her own determination not to get involved with another man, she found herself intrigued by him and wanting to know him better.

After the Danes and Peter Moss had hurried off to

freshen up and change prior to meeting their mainland
visitors, Chad too had to rush off, having received a call
summoning him to a sick child in one of the luxury apartment blocks.

'How about meeting me for dinner?' he asked as he
turned to go. 'There's a nice place on the beachfront . . . the
Prawn Basket. Have you tried it?'

'No, I haven't.' She tried not to show how ridiculously
pleased she felt. In fact, because she was annoyed with
herself for feeling pleased at all, she made sure that her
response was decidedly offhand. 'What time?'

'Meet you there around seven. Patients permitting. Grab
one of the outside tables if you get there first.'

'Will do.' Seven . . . That gave her plenty of time to put
her feet up before changing for dinner.

Chad arrived twenty minutes late. She had ordered
a multi-coloured cocktail and was sipping it through a straw
when he slid into the seat opposite. She had chosen a table
on the balcony, overlooking the beach, with an unimpeded
view across the calm shining water.

'Had a last minute call,' Chad apologised as a waiter
hastened over to take his order. 'One of the drawbacks of
being a one-man band. You're always on call, even when
you're off-duty.'

She nodded, understanding what being on call meant
better than he imagined. She paused to wonder why he was
bothering to point out the drawbacks of his profession to
her, a casual acquaintance, a mere model as far as he was
concerned, and one who would soon be out of his life; but
she shrugged the thought aside. Most likely it was just a
passing remark.

As they sipped their cocktails, they chatted easily about

the adventures of the afternoon, sharing a laugh at poor
Peter Moss's expense, and Gemma felt a pleasant warmth
creeping through her. She decided she would be silly to
dwell on motives or guilt feelings or on whether she would
ever see Chad again after tonight, or whether she even
wanted to . . . Why not just enjoy his company while she
had it, and not think about anything at all?

She gazed past him, contentedly breathing in the hot,
humid, sweet-smelling air. The coconut palms lining the
beach were silhouetted now against a brilliant orange sky,
and the still water beyond was like a sheet of gold.
Paradise, she thought. This is paradise. Or it could be
. . . for some.

She sobered as she recalled Chad's wife, who had died
here on this very island—died tragically, and perhaps
unnecessarily—and she wondered anew how Chad could
have found the strength of will to come and work here,
after what had happened. She could understand him
wanting to see a more efficient medical service on the
island, but for him to take on the job himself . . .
Admirable as it was, it puzzled her a little. For a doctor of
Chad's undoubted ability—a relatively young man
apparently at the height of his career—to give up a thriving
mainland practice to come and work in what was virtually
a backwater, in surroundings that must be filled with
unhappy memories . . . Gemma shook her head. In many
ways, it didn't make sense.

'What are you thinking?' Chad's voice cut into her
thoughts.

She caught her breath, faintly startled at the question,
surprised that Chad had even noticed that her mind was
elsewhere, let alone that he should care what her thoughts
might be. How could she admit that she had been thinking

about *him*? And about his wife, about whom he never talked? Her mind raced to her rescue.

'Chad, I noticed your painting down in the cabin this afternoon, I liked it very much.'

He gave a burst of laughter. 'That's kind of you, Gemma.'

She looked at him quickly, her brow puckering. 'What are you laughing at? Have I said something amusing?'

'Not at all. It's just nice to know you're not invincible.'

'What do you mean?' she demanded.

'I mean that I'm prepared to concede that you're an outstanding model and a top-notch life-saver and a first-rate swimmer, and I've no doubt you're a superb water-skier, windsurfer and snorkeller. But a top-notch art critic you most certainly are not.'

'I don't pretend to be,' she said with a grin. 'Anyway, I didn't say it was great art,' she added with a mock pout. 'I just said I liked it.'

'So you did. Sorry. I guess I'm over-conscious of my shortcomings.'

'Is that because your wife was such a brilliant artist?' she hazarded, deciding on the spur of the moment to risk the withering 'Dr Rivers cold treatment' in order to let him know that she knew about his wife. It made her uncomfortable pretending she knew nothing about her when she did. She felt it put Chad at an unfair disadvantage.

At his sharp look, she added quickly, 'Melanie mentioned what happened. You don't mind, do you?'

He shrugged, the sharpness fading from his eyes. 'It's no secret. I guess I've just found it easier not to talk about it. I still get angry . . . What happened was such a tragic waste of a talented, vibrantly healthy young life.'

She looked at him musingly. In a way, he sounded more like a sorrowful doctor than a grieving husband. Was it to cover the very real grief he must be feeling inside?

'I still believe that if there had been a doctor or an efficient nurse on call that day, Roxanne just might have been saved,' he muttered, frowning into his cocktail. 'Now the island has someone on call twenty-four hours a day—I've made sure of that. I've also trained the resort staff in first aid and resuscitation procedures. Prompt action in these cases is vital.'

'Especially with the Chironex,' Gemma agreed, uttering the words without thinking. As the scientific name rolled off her tongue, she realised how incongruous it must sound, dropping with such ease from the lips of a supposed fashion model. Noting the way Chad's brow shot up, she hastened to explain the slip away. 'Melanie said that's what it was. And I remember reading somewhere about the types of box jellyfish before I came up here.' Let him think she'd read about it in travel brochures, rather than in her medical textbooks.

'You knew about the Chironex . . . and yet this afternoon you jumped into the water, in the middle of summer, without a second thought.' Chad's eyes flickered in the misty golden light, and she saw tiny pinpoints of amber darting about in the grey.

She wasn't sure if that was a criticism—or an expression of reluctant respect. Or was he thinking how stupid she was? A crazy, foolhardy southerner, who acted without thinking, without wearing suitable protection!

'I'll take more care in future,' she promised, and because she knew this conversation must be paining him, no matter how well he might be hiding it, she changed the subject. 'And have you painted other things besides seascapes,

Chad? Landscapes, still-life studies, portraits?'

'Portraits?' He threw back his head in a gust of laughter. 'You have to be able to draw faces and figures to do a portrait, and I'm hopeless at anything on two legs. No, just landscapes and seascapes . . . I know my limits.'

'Do you spend much time painting?' she asked curiously.

'Not these days.' He shrugged.'I seem to have lost the urge.' He was looking past her now, a remote expression in his eyes., and Gemma had the feeling he was barely noticing the fiery sky or the vivid amber sheen on the water. He's thinking of his wife, she mused, aware of a strange poignancy at the thought. He still misses her, even after two and a half years . . . He must have loved her very much.

She said gently, 'You should take it up again, Chad. You're very good. Not brilliant, mind you,' she added teasingly, to lighten the air. 'Well, not *yet*. But you definitely show promise.'

He tilted his head at her. 'You're not afraid to give an opinion, expert or not, are you, Gemma Hayes? What are you trying to do? Convince a guy he's got some talent? I'm just a raw amateur.'

'With a raw talent you should develop,' she persisted.

He looked at her quickly, and there was an unfathomable expression in his eyes. 'My wife said that once,' he admitted at length, and then he smiled suddenly, his lips stretching, bringing an immediate softening to his features. Gemma took his remark as a compliment and smiled back, flushing slightly because it was the first time Chad had mentioned his wife without being prompted. Was she beginning to break through the iron reserve he wrapped around himself?

She asked cautiously, 'Wouldn't she be disappointed

that you're denying your raw talent?'

Chad spread his hands. 'Disappointed maybe, not surprised.' It was an enigmatic answer. Did he mean that his wife would have *expected* him to give up his painting in deference to her memory? His tone held more dryness than sentiment. It was hard to tell what he meant. 'Besides, 'I've had other priorities in my spare time,' Chad added with a shrug.

She looked at him questioningly, her dark eyes encouraging, willing him to tell her about it. After a moment's hesitation, he did.

'I've been preparing a booklet on marine stingers of the Great Barrier Reef . . . involving mostly underwater research.' His gazed drifted away, out over the gleaming water. 'It's being sponsored by the University of Queensland, who plan to circulate it to every island and coastal region along the tropical Pacific coast.'

When he paused, she begged gently, 'Tell me about it, Chad. What does it cover?'

'It gives detailed descriptions of all the venomous creatures in these waters, and covers treatment of stings, resuscitation technology, and methods of protection. There'll be diagrams and photographs . . .'

'Your own?'

'Mostly. As well as some from official files. I finished it last week, as a matter of fact, and it's being prepared for printing now.' There was a rumble of satisfaction in his voice. But underlying it was a poignant note. Because the booklet was coming out too late to help Roxanne?

Gemma asked no further questions. Instead, they discussed the menu, and while they were tucking into the exquisitely tasty tiger prawns, they talked about inconsequential things. Until Chad invited carelessly, 'Tell me about yourself, Gemma. What family do you have?'

She swallowed. Once she started talking about herself, how long would it be before the truth came tumbling out? She didn't feel ready to end her masquerade just yet. She still wasn't altogether secure in Chad's friendship, and she had no wish to win him over so easily. If she could get by without telling any deliberate lies, she would keep up the pretence just a little longer . . .

Briefly she told him that she had a father who was semi-retired—she didn't mention that he was a doctor, and rushed on before Chad could ask any questions—and a mother who did voluntary work at a hospital, and three sisters, all older than herself, one who had married a year ago and was now expecting her first child, the other two working in the city, one in finance, the other in computing.

'And are your sisters blonde and beautiful like you?' Chad asked, eyeing her over the rim of his glass.

'Better-looking,' she quipped. She could sense what was coming next. Something along the lines of, And yet you were the only one who chose a modelling career . . .

She forestalled him. 'They both have steady boyfriends and they're both talking of settling down soon, like Lucy.'

'And what about you?' Chad's brow rose fractionally. 'You mentioned once that you'd come up here to get away from a man . . .'

So he'd remembered that slip of hers . . . She chewed on her lip and nodded. While she was debating how much she should tell Chad about Jonathan, he shot another question at her.

'Is it all over between you?'

The question surprised her. Why would he want to know that? Why should he even care? Idle curiosity?

She looked down at her glass. 'Yes . . . it's over.' She

paused, swallowing. 'We've known each other for years.
In fact . . . we were engaged to be married. I——' Again
she hesitated, seeing danger ahead if she wanted to keep up
her pretence. 'I broke it off before I came up here because
we didn't see eye to eye about—about certain things.' Be
satisfied with that, Chad Rivers, she pleaded silently, but
without much hope.

As she glanced up at him, she caught a metallic glint in
the grey. 'He didn't like the kind of work you were doing?'
he asked shrewdly. 'He wanted you to give it up?'

She swallowed. Perceptive of you, Dr Rivers. Even if
you were thinking of a different profession altogether . . .

She raised her glass to her lips. Well, now, Gemma, let's
see how good you are at equivocating . . . 'That was
basically it,' she admitted cautiously. And it was true
enough. Jonathan *didn't* like her work—her *medical*
career—because of the demands it made on her time and
energy and the way it inconvenienced *him*. And he *had*
wanted her to give it up. The fact that she was thinking
about medicine, and Chad was thinking about modelling,
was irrelevant. The principle was the same.

'And you wouldn't,' Chad probed. There was barely an
inflection in his tone, as if he already knew the answer, and
just wanted her to confirm it.

'No, I wouldn't,' she said, and sighed. 'I guess I just
didn't love him enough, or I'd have tried harder to find a
solution. It's over . . . and that's all there is to it.' Why was
she so anxious for Chad to know that? 'Jonathan wants
one thing, and I want another. Simple as that.'

'So you're not missing him, then?' Now there was a
faint smile tugging at Chad's lips, a teasing glint in his eye.
How seriously did he want to know the answer to that
one? she found herself wondering.

Because she was still hiding things from Chad, she tried to be honest here. 'I'm surprised at how little I *am* missing him.' She felt her cheeks glowing as she made the admission. 'I guess I must have done the right thing,' she added with a shrug. 'Let's not talk about Jonathan,' she begged. 'Tell me something about *you*.'

For a moment she thought the cold treatment was descending again. But then she saw the start of another smile. 'You've been honest with me, so now it's my turn . . . huh?'

On the brink of nodding, she shook her head instead. 'I shouldn't have asked,' she said, suddenly contrite. Chad had suffered a very real tragedy. In comparison, her broken engagement seemed a trivial topic of conversation. As for being honest . . . She felt a guilty flush warming her cheeks. She hadn't been honest with Chad at all . . . not really. True, she had told him about Jonathan. But she had done nothing to correct Chad's misassumptions about her *work*. He still thought she was a model!

'Let's go for a walk along the beach,' Chad said suddenly, and she glimpsed a softening warmth in his eyes that hadn't been there a moment ago, even when he'd smiled. It gave her a faint jolt, and she didn't trust herself to speak for a moment. She reached for her bag to hide her face from his, and it was only when she heard him scrape back his chair that she risked glancing up again, smiling so that she didn't have to speak. She still wasn't sure she could trust her voice to be perfectly cool and normal.

As she preceded Chad down the timber steps to the beach, she silently berated herself. She was acting like a nervous schoolgirl! Which was pretty mind-boggling, since Gemma Hayes had never been nervous of any man in her life! The trouble was, she had been going out with one man for so long that she was over-reacting now, just because another man was showing a spark of interest in her.

You'll have to do better than that, Gemma, my girl, a small voice scoffed. Think of all the young men who have tried to make passes at you over the years. Think of all the doctors and male patients who have given you the glad eye in these past few months, ring on your finger or not. Dr Chad Rivers isn't the first man to notice you, so don't pretend he is.

So why was she getting so jumpy?

It's because you're a free woman now, she concluded. That's what's making you nervous. What else could it be?

She kicked off her shoes, wanting to feel the warm sand on the soles of her feet and trickling between her toes, hoping it might help to drive away her tension. But Chad's presence at her side made it difficult to return to her normal calm. She was acutely aware, without even looking at him, of the panther-like grace of his stride, of the occasional brush of his bare arm against hers, making the fine hairs on the surface of her skin leap upright as though stung, of the fact that the top of her head barely reached his shoulder . . .

When had she last felt this aware of a man?

Gemma, you might as well face it, she thought. For the first time since Jonathan, *you* are interested in a man. And you'd jolly well better not stay interested, at least not for too long. You have your career in Sydney to think of. As for Chad, to him you're merely a diversion. His heart still belongs to his lost wife. He *wants* to feel close to her . . . it's probably the real reason he came here.

She sighed, without knowing precisely why.

'Glorious night,' Chad observed, breaking the silence

that had fallen between them.

'Magical,' she agreed, hoping he wouldn't read anything into the word; hoping he hadn't been reading her
thoughts.

It *was* a magical evening. The moon was rising, casting a
silvery shimmer across the water, and it was very still and
quiet on the beach, the only sound being the gentle
'swoosh' now and then as a wave kissed the sand.

And then a familiar sound pierced the air. Chad's
pocket beeper!'

'Damn!' he swore. 'We're going to have to go back. I'm
sorry.'

'No need to apologise,' she said easily, thinking how
often it had happened to her. She saw him glance down at
her gratefully, and as their eyes met the air between them
seemed suddenly to be alive with static electricity. She
caught her breath, aware of his eyes glowing in the
darkness, aware of his closeness, aware that her head was
spinning, even while her mind was crying out, It's just the
balmy tropical night . . . the moonlight . . . being here
alone in the darkness with a man who isn't Jonathan . . .
get a grip on yourself, girl!

She saw him looking down at her, and his eyes were
glittering like diamonds. Was he laughing at her? Had he
been reading her mind, after all?

'You look very kissable,' he said and, before she could
react, his lips were on hers. As kisses went, there wasn't
much to it. His lips had barely touched hers before they
were gone again. The most chaste of kisses, without heat,
without passion, promising nothing, demanding nothing.
And yet it left her breathless—more breathless than she
would have cared to admit. Anxious not to show it, she
took refuge in banter, scolding him with mock severity,

'Dr Rivers! You have a patient waiting . . .'

Unabashed, he grinned and caught her hand. 'My limousine awaits. Shall we go? I'll drop you off on the way.'

'Limousine?' She spluttered with laughter. 'Since when do people have limousines on this island?' She had to run to keep up with him.

He dragged her up some steps to the road. '*Volià*!'

'Oh, Chad, you idiot!' she gasped. His limousine was a small four-wheel mini-moke—a favourite method of transport on the island.

'Hop in. There's a suggestion I'd like to put to you before I drop you off.'

'A suggestion?' She looked at him enquiringly, her heart giving a tiny leap. A suggestion to . . . meet again, perhaps? Or . . . An unaccustomed doubt quivered through her. Or *not* to meet again . . . to stop before anything started? She held her breath, masking her scampering thoughts with a deceptive calm.

As the engine coughed to life and the tiny red vehicle bounced forwards, Chad asked, 'How about putting off your scuba-diving excursion tomorrow and coming sailing with me instead?'

She swallowed, aware of a wave of relief. 'You're going out sailing again tomorrow?' she hedged, not wanting to appear too anxious.

'It's Sunday and I have the whole day off. Why not? If we leave early enough, we could sail to the Outer Barrier. I can promise you some spectacular sights.'

'Oh, that would be great!' This time her reaction, her enthusiasm, was spontaneous. She would far rather go to the Reef with Chad than with a bunch of scuba-diving strangers.

'That's settled, then.

She wished she could read *his* thoughts right now. You hide them well, Dr Rivers, she congratulated him silently. Are you just inviting me out of the kindness of your heart? Or is there more to it?

'Think you could be at the marina by six in the morning?' he asked.

'Why so late?' she quipped.

He grinned, and slammed his foot on the brakes, bringing the moke to a halt. 'Here's your bure. See you in the morning, then . . . I'll bring Melanie's stinger suit for you to wear so we can go diving out on the reef. Sleep well!'

'Thanks for a great day, Chad.' And for a magical evening, she added silently. She stood and watched him go, the breeze ruffling his hair, the moonlight flashing on his teeth, giving him an irrepressibly boyish look.

Now you're getting fanciful, she admonished herself with an ironic smile. Anyone less irrepressibly boyish than Dr Chad Rivers you'd be hard put to it to find. But he *was* starting to let his hair down a bit. He *was* showing that he had a warmer, more human side, and that it wasn't reserved solely for his patients.

'I'll bring Melanie's stinger suit,' he had offered. She stood a moment longer, her lips pursed. When would Chad pick it up from Melanie? It would be too early to pick it up in the morning. Did he intend visiting the Danes tonight, after he had finished with his patient? Would Nick be there? Or would Melanie be home alone . . .

She caught herself up sharply. You're jealous! she accused herself in shocked dismay. It was a disturbing thought. She had never been jealous of any man in her life, not even Jonathan . . . And this was a man she barely knew, and hadn't the remotest claim on. It was crazy!

'You're not a well person, Gemma Hayes,' she reproached herself with a comical shake of her head, trying to joke herself out of what she knew was sheer idiocy. Being jealous of a man she'd only known a couple of days and would probably never see again after this weekend! 'You'd better do as the doctor ordered and get a good night's sleep. You need it!'

CHAPTER SIX

GEMMA arrived at the marina ten minutes early, and Chad was already on board, warming up the motor.

'Good morning,' he greeted her as she joined him. 'You must have had a good night's sleep. You're early.'

'Oh, I did,' she lied. In truth, she had tossed and turned for most of the night, her thoughts jumbled, leading nowhere, resolving nothing. She had tried to think of Jonathan, but Chad's face had kept intervening, haunting her after his teasing grin, the way his eyes so often turned from grey to silver, the memory of his warm lips brushing hers . . . Not even a proper kiss! It had been so swift, so unassuming, it was a joke she even remembered it at all. Did *he*? Probably not. Only a fool would read anything into it. Or into his invitation today.

'Pop your things down below,' Chad said, noticing the bag in her hand. 'You look as if you've come prepared for anything this time.'

She grinned. 'Towel, swimsuit, change of clothes, spare pair of shoes for walking on the coral, and a hat.'

'Well done. And I brought Melanie's stinger suit for you.' He didn't say when he had picked it up, or mention whether Melanie and Nick had both been home at the time. 'As soon as you come up again, we'll go. You'll find a lifejacket down below—put it on. Where we're going today, conditions won't be as placid as they were yesterday.'

Within minutes she had dropped her bag, donned the lifejacket, and rejoined him, and a couple of minutes later they were away. A faint golden mist hung over the harbour. It was warm and humid even at this early hour, and the water was glassy-smooth, sure signs of another hot, sticky day.

This time it was she who helped Chad hurl the sails when they reached the passage. She had sailed before and knew what to do. She saw him nod approvingly, and her cheeks glowed with pleasure.

It was a glow that remained with her for the rest of the day, a day that she could only have described as idyllic. Once they left the serene island-studded Whitsunday Passage behind and headed north-east in the direction of the Outer Barrier, the wind strengthened and they zipped through the water at an exhilarating speed.

All around lay coral atolls and tropical islands of breath-catching beauty. She stood at the rail, comfortably braced against the gentle rise and fall of the deck, breathing in the salty air and enjoying the occasional dollops of spray that slapped on to her face and neck and bare brown legs. She had worn her shorts today, and it made her smile now when she recalled how coy she had been yesterday about baring her legs in front of Chad.

And now here she was alone with him, miles from anywhere, and yet she felt no coyness at all. In fact, she was savouring every second in his company . . .

She heard Chad's deep voice at her ear. 'You look like a proud goddess of the sea, standing there with your golden hair streaming behind you and that enigmatic smile on your lips. Care to tell me what the smile signifies?'

She turned to face him, her heart jumping slightly when she realised how close he was; he must have turned on the auto-helm so that he could leave the wheel.

'It just means that I'm enjoying myself,' she said, striving at lightness. No point getting all earnest and sentimental and confessing that she was enjoying *his* company as much as their surroundings . . . It could give him the wrong idea. She wasn't looking for anything from Chad—either consolation for her break-up from Jonathan, or a fleeting holiday affair . . . brief, meaningless flings weren't Gemma's style. And she most certainly wasn't looking for anything deeper—for any kind of serious entanglement. In a week or two she would be committing herself to a full-time medical practice in Sydney. The last thing she wanted was another man complicating her life.

Not that Chad would be looking for anything 'deeper'. To him, she was just someone passing through. And she mustn't forget that she was also, as far as Chad was concerned, a model. And Chad had told Melanie, very emphatically, that he would never become seriously involved with a model. It didn't matter that she *wasn't* a model. Chad thought that she was—that was the point. And yet he was still seeking her out. So what he had in mind was no more than a bit of harmless fun . . . if that.

'You've stopped smiling,' Chad complained. 'You're not wishing you were here with . . . someone else, I hope?'

She looked at him quickly. 'If you mean with Jonathan, the answer is no. I told you, that's all over.'

His sunglasses hid any change of expression in his eyes. She couldn't tell what he was thinking, or even if he believed her. She shifted her gaze, looking out over the gently swelling turquoise waves, a faint frown puckering her brow. If he felt he could ask her personal questions, why should she back away from asking him one?

'And what about you?' she asked, without turning to face him. 'I guess you still miss your wife?'

'For a moment she thought he wasn't going to answer She didn't look round to see if the withering Dr Rivers chill had descended again. Nor did she retract the question. She just stood there, waiting. Hoping he would answer.

At length, he did. 'I think about her. Often.' There was a hardness in his tone, as if to mask any sentiment. And then he added, 'But it's mostly angry, guilty thoughts . . .'

'Guilty?' Now she did turn to face him. 'Why should you feel guilty? You weren't even here when . . . at the time.'

'That's right . . . I wasn't here with her.' His voice hardened with bitter self-reproach. 'A husband's place is supposed to be with his wife . . . isn't it?' The question was laced with cynicism. 'But I was too busy. I was often too busy to spend time with my wife . . .'

A silence fell between them; his words, heavy with irony and self-reproach, lingering in the air. Gemma thought that was all he was going to say, that he was retreating again behind his protective shield. Not knowing what to say, but wanting him to know that she understood, she reached out involuntarily and touched his arm.

He made no sign that he had felt the gesture; his profile could have been carved of stone. But a moment later she was surprised, and moved, when he went on, his eyes intent on the stretch of water ahead, his tone more reflective now than grim.

'Roxanne had her painting, her exhibitions, her close circle of friends . . . she was as wrapped up in her own work as I was in mine. Art was her *raison d'être*, you might say—it filled her whole life. She didn't want domesticity—and that was fine; we employed a housekeeper.

She didn't want children, either—and I went along with that as well. When you're both leading full, busy lives, you'd be selfish and cruel to have children . . .'

A new note had crept into his voice, hardness, a remoteness that puzzled Gemma. Had Chad secretly wanted children? Or was he simply regretting his selfishness, now that it was too late?

Suddenly she saw Chad tense, and make a grab for the wheel. It was only then she noticed the group of coral cays looming ahead. She grinned.

'Nice to know you're being vigilant. I don't fancy being shipwrecked right out here. It would be a long way to have to swim for help.'

His features relaxed as he shot her an answering grin. 'I thought you were going to let *me* do any rescuing next time. Have you always been this fiercely independent?'

'Always. It must be having sisters instead of brothers. You get used to sticking up for yourself because there are no boys to stick up for you. We're all pretty tough, come to think of it.' Her sisters had had to compete in a predominantly man's world too—the world of business and finance.

'I'm almost tempted to push you overboard just to hear you yell out "help",' Chad threatened.

She gave a mock shudder. 'Help!' she yelped. 'There! You won't push me overboard now, will you?'

'Unfair,' Chad accused. 'Your day will come.'

Their playfulness came easily and naturally . . . and it provided welcome relief too, from the seriousness of a moment ago. Gemma felt a new closeness to Chad. It was almost frightening how close, and how comfortable, she did feel with him. Did he feel the same way? He certainly *looked* more at ease than she had ever seen him before.

'Outer Barrier Reef ahoy!' Chad pointed ahead. 'Let's get those sails down!'

'Aye aye, sir.'

Moments later she was staring, fascinated and wide-eyed, at the enchanting world which lay before them. Coral, light brown, brick-red, purple-green, stretched as far as the eye could see. The outer Barrier . . . the largest expanse of coral reef in the world: a reef criss-crossed by a maze of channels, some dead-ends, others leading to the open sea.

'Drop anchor!' Chad shouted.

'Aye aye, Captain, sir!'

The boat swung around until it was perfectly positioned, lying still in the crystal-clear water, over a sandy bottom, but only about five metres from the edge of the coral, a dark mass rippling below the surface.

'How about a bit of skin-diving before lunch?' Chad suggested.

'Suits me.'

'You'll find Melanie's stinger suit down below.'

'Are you wearing one, too?' she asked.

He nodded. 'After you . . . unless you'd like me to come down with you.'

'After me, by all means,' she said, beating a hasty retreat.

When they both met again on desk, they were wearing identical electric-blue suits.

'His and hers,' Gemma commented, her brow rising as she glanced up at Chad. 'You must have chosen them together,' she said, turning the question into a playful quip.

Chad looked amused. 'Sheer coincidence.' He handed her a pair of flippers and a snorkel mask. 'Nick has an aqua-coloured one.'

'I guess he doesn't get a chance to wear his,' Gemma said, wondering, and hating herself for it, if Chad had ever sought Melanie out while Nick was busy working.

'Not often . . . he's a worker, Nick. Gives his life's blood. Which is why I coaxed him away from the island yesterday. I know how he loves to sail . . . He'd have enjoyed coming out with us today, only he was on duty at the resort.'

'And Melanie?' Gemma asked involuntarily, as she pulled on her flippers.

'Melanie agreed to be on call for me today, since I was coming all the way out here. She knows she can always contact me by radio if she needs any advice. But I doubt if she will . . . she's a very capable nurse. I can trust her to deal with most emergencies. In the event of anything really serious arising, it's only minutes to the mainland by air. Melanie knows that.'

Had Melanie minded being left on call while Chad spent the day with another woman? Gemma pondered a moment, and then dismissed the thought with an impatient shrug. Why should the girl mind? What right had Melanie, a married woman, to be jealous of Chad Rivers' women friends? For that matter, what right had she, Gemma Hayes, to speculate about either of them?

'So you're stuck with just me,' Chad said, grinning. Gemma held her breath, half hoping he might add, Anyway, I wanted you all to myself. When he didn't, she released her breath slowly, feeling relieved, in a way. It was the kind of suggestive, meaningless platitude that Peter Moss would have made. Coming from Chad, she would have wanted to believe it . . . and that could be a very foolish thing for her to do.

'Ready to go?' she asked, pulling on her mask.

He nodded as he pulled on his own.

A moment later Gemma found herself in another world, suspended in crystal space, in water that was so clear that it didn't seem to be there. She became completely absorbed in the fantastic variety of colours and shapes of the living reef. As magnificent as the corals were, it was the fish that especially fascinated her. Red, orange, brown, green purple, brilliant silver, bright electric-blue, some spotted, others striped, others with filmy fins, they were there in their thousands, living on, in and among the coral.

When they reboarded the boat, Chad produced from the galley an enticing lunch of tropical fruit and salad, and for a while they lazed on the sun-drenched deck, eating, drinking, and enthusing about the beauties they had seen.

As the sun rose higher in the sky, Gemma realised she was becoming increasingly aware of Chad's near-naked frame lying sprawled out on the deck beside her. They had long since discarded their stifling stinger suits, and now wore only their swimsuits: in Chad's case, a tiny strip of grey fabric that was almost as provocative as if he had worn nothing at all; not that her own scanty white bikini was, if she only knew it, any less seductive.

The hot sun was beating down on the deck, the steamy heat pervading her limbs, filling her with a wicked sense of abandonment, of simmering excitement. She couldn't resist flicking an occasional furtive glance at Chad's powerful thighs, and at his bronzed arms draped across his well-muscled chest, nothing with hazy pleasure the crisp golden hair that sprouted in silky profusion from his deeply tanned skin.

When, without warning, Chad rolled over on to his side, her eyeslashes fluttered hastily downwards, their shadow spreading fanlike across her flushed cheeks.

'Surrounded by beauty,' Chad murmured with a contented sigh. 'Who could ask for more?'

As she peeped at him from under her lashes, Gemma felt something catch in her throat. Because he was not looking at the reef now, but at her.

He reached out and touched her cheek, brushing his fingertips over her satin-smooth skin. 'Your skin is like the softest velvet,' he said almost reverently. And then he said something that was anything *but* reverent. 'I wonder if the rest of you is the same . . .'

He let his fingers trail lightly downwards, tracing the smooth line of her chin and the graceful sweep of her throat sliding on down over her creamy skin to pause, tantalisingly, just above the swell of her breast

'I wonder . . .' He repeated huskily, and there was a questioning look in his eyes.

His touch was sending hot flames licking through her already fiery body, and she was conscious of a rushing in her ears, as if she were still swimming underwater. Her gaze became riveted to his naked chest. In the sultry heat, his smooth, tanned skin was glistening with a film of moisture, and she felt an almost overwhelming urge to reach out and test its texture, the way he was doing with hers.

'I'm right here,' she heard herself inviting, in a husky voice she hardly recognised as her own, 'if you're interested in finding out . . .'

Dear heaven, Gemma, just listen to you . . . You sound positively wanton! You've never been the wanton type before—what's got into you? Even during medical school, when you were trying to prove to everyone that you were a liberated woman, equal to any man . . . even when all those virile medical students and resident doctors were chasing you among the cadavers, you never slept around. You've never even slept with Jonathan! What in the world are you doing, offering Dr Rivers a free rein on your body, for heaven's sake? A man who still believes you're a model—and you know how he thinks of models. As beneath contempt! So what do you think his intentions are here? Don't imagine they're sincere and honourable—the man's just playing with you for his own amusement . . .

He was playing with her now . . . *literally*, she realised dazedly, as his fingers drifted lower, slipping under the scanty white fabric of her bikini bra, seeking the rosy peak underneath. His closeness was like a drug, lulling her into euphoria. As his fingers found what they were seeking, and gently teased it to throbbing tautness, she felt tiny, convulsive shudders quivering through her, and it was all she could do not to press herself frantically against him.

He's just playing with you, she repeated desperately. He just wants to prove to himself that models are as worthless and degenerate as he's always suspected! And your wanton behaviour will be doing nothing to convince him otherwise!

With a gasp she rolled away from him, and sat up. 'I was only kidding,' she panted, her dark eyes smouldering with mingled passion and self-reproach. 'You didn't have to take me at my word! It—it must be this steamy tropical atmosphere . . . I—I don't know what came over me!' She felt too mortified to look Chad in the eye.

'You're not such a sophisticate as you'd have people believe, are you, Gemma?' Chad observed softly. He didn't sound peeved—quite the reverse, in fact. He sounded amused, if anything! But she didn't dare look at him to check, because, mortification aside, she was still shaking from the heady emotion that had swept over her a moment ago, and she was afraid it might sweep over her again if her eyes should happen to stray just at the moment to his bronzed, sinewy body.

'I think it's time we explored the Reef,' Clad proposed, and she wholeheartedly agreed with him. Pulling on their rubber-soled shoes to protect their feet from the sharp coral, and donning shirts, hats and sunglasses to protect themselves from the beating sun—and from each other? Gemma speculated ruefully—they lowered the rubber dinghy, pulled it up on to the coral, and spent the next hour or so fossicking for shells along the Reef—until Chad looked up at the sky with a slight frown.

'I don't like the look of that sky. We'd better get back to the boat. I'd like to hear a weather forecast.'

Gemma glanced up. All she could see to indicate any kind of change in the weather were a few thin, high clouds in an otherwise clear blue sky. Surely nothing to worry about?

She waited while Chad ducked below. When he reported back, it was more what he didn't say than what he did that caused her a faint twinge of alarm. 'We'd better start heading back. We could have some strong winds down this way before long, with some rain. Nothing to be concerned about—we'll be back in harbour long before the worst of the weather hits us. It's up north at the moment, hours away.'

'I'm ready when you are.' She refrained from asking if by 'strong winds' he meant a gale . . . or even a cyclone. If Chad said they would be back in harbour in time, that was all right by her. There was something about Chad that inspired confidence—quite apart from the passion he inspired, she reflected, aware of a flare of heat along her cheekbones. She felt safe with him. Safe and protected. Had she ever felt 'safe and protected' with Jonathan? She paused to wonder. She had felt 'comfortable' with him, certainly. She had trusted and respected him and had always known she could rely on him. But *Safe*? *Protected*? They were new sensations to Gemma. Sensations she had never expected to have, or expected to need.

Neither spoke much on the trip back. The wind was steadily picking up strength, although it was still warm, and as the boat cut through the waves Chad needed all his concentration to judge the wind's strength and direction. He insisted that Gemma wear a safety harness if she were to remain on deck, whch she insisted on doing; she was eager to stand by so that she could give Chad a helping hand when needed.

She noticed that a layer of cloud was now blanketing the sky, and that the surface of the water was disturbed and slate-grey, rather than its usual serene and sunny blue.

By the time they entered the Whitsunday Passage, heavy clouds were scudding low over the grey, and the wind was whipping up short, choppy waves and dumping them on to the rock-hewn shores of the passing islands.

And then the rain started, a few drops at first, then a steady downpour, running warm and liquid down their bare arms and cheeks and hissing on to the deck.

'Nearly there!' Chad shouted. He grinned at her. 'If Zara Magatelli could only see you now!'

'Zara Magatelli?' Gamma groaned inwardly. Of course . . . to Chad she was still one of Zara Magatelli's models! And Zara Magatelli's models would simply never be seen with their hair plastered to their heads and with soaking wet shirts clinging to their bodies, making them look for all the world like drowned rats! 'I'm on holiday, remember?' she reminded him with a flash of spirit. 'I'm not treading a catwalk now. Models aren't so very different from other people, you know, Dr Rivers. They do like to relax and let their hair down occasionally, when they're not working.'

She expected a cynical reply along the lines of, Not the models I know, but he surprised her.

'You're certainly let *your* hair down,' he retorted, grin widening. 'Literally. I've never seen hair so flattened. And you look irresistible. Good enough to eat!'

She flushed, her flesh prickling at the memory of his fingers railing over her body, but she managed to repress the sensation, and tossed him an answering grin. Pleased that Chad was able to joke at last about a subject which previously he had wanted only to deride.

'You look rather flattened yourself,' she flung back, eyeing his dripping hair. Below it, his suntanned face was gleaming with water, tiny silvery droplets clinging to his lashes, and she felt like telling him that he was looking pretty irresistible too, only she got cold feet and mocked him instead. 'If your patients could only see you now!'

Something shimmered in his grey eyes, before they snapped away. 'If my patients are ever going to see me again, I'd better concentrate.'

That was the first indication she had that Chad was more concerned than he had been making out. She tossed an anxious look over the grey, restless waves. The light was very poor now, and the islands were disappearing one by one behind the curtain of rain. Coconut palms were just visible along the shoreline of the island closest to them, tossing uneasily in the steadily increasing wind.

They lapsed into silence as they concentrated on the job

in hand, and twenty minutes later Chad successfully negotiated the narrow passage into the harbour. It was only when the boat was safely moored that Chad told Gemma the full facts.

'There's a cyclone on the way.' He went on to explain that it was bearing down from the Coral Sea with torrential rain and wind gusts of over a hundred and fifty kilometres an hour, and was now only a couple of hours away.

Gemma wasn't surprised. All the signs had been there, and it was the right time of year. December through to April was the cyclone season, the time when the giant, capricious storms were born in the warm tropical seas. She felt an uneasy knot growing in her stomach. She was recalling Cyclone Tracy, which had devastated the city of Darwin a few years back. What damage would a cyclone do to an exposed coastal resort like this one?

Together they secured the boat and removed any loose objects from the deck, noting that other boat owners were frenziedly rushing around doing the same. Afterwards they gathered up their things and hastened to Chad's tiny red mini-moke, the rain beating down on their hunched shoulders, the howling wind stealing their breath away and bringing stinging tears to their eyes.

'I'll take you back to your bure,' Chad shouted, waving her into the front seat. 'You can change into some dry clothes while I whip back to my house and secure the storm shutters. Then I'll be back.'

'Back?' she echoed, aware of an odd flutter inside. Did he mean he was coming back to join *her*? Or merely coming back to the resort?

'Back to pick you up. I'll take you with me to the resort—I could be needed there tonight,' Chad shouted as the tiny buggy bounced along the narrow road. The wind was moaning through the coconut trees, bending them alarmingly, occasionally ripping off fronds and sending them whirling through the air. 'Got a raincoat?'

She nodded absently. She was thinking that if Chad was going to be needed tonight, she could well be needed too. After all, she was a doctor too. She wouldn't waste his time telling him now—they were only seconds from her bure—but she would when he came back to pick her up. Her little masquerade had pretty well served its purpose by now. Chad, she sensed with satisfaction, and with a pleasurable warmth as well, seemed to have come to genuinely like her—and she sensed a grudging respect for her too—and she knew that, for a man with such a chip on his shoulder about models, that respect, that liking, couldn't have come easily.

'Then wear it.' Chad's voice cut through her thoughts. 'Now, in you go . . . .' The mini-moke skidded to a halt. 'And don't you worry . . . the cyclone's some distance away yet. It might even fizzle out before it gets this far, with a bit of luck.'

'Oh, I'm not worried,' she said at once. She was more worried about *him*, driving to his isolated home in the bush in this appalling wind and the equally hazardous rain.

'Doesn't anything ever rattle you?' Chad shook his head admiringly. Or was it in exasperation? She couldn't be sure.

'Yes—spiders,' she shot back with a grin.

As the mini-moke leapt away, a gust of wind whipped Chad's voice back to her. 'Stay inside until I get back. You'll be quite safe there—those bures are very solidly built.'

She stood watching him go, chewing on her lip as the little red moke vanished into the swirling rain, buffeted by alarming blasts of wind. She knew he didn't have far to go, but the road leading to his house was, she had gathered from remarks he'd made, barely more than a track lined with trees and thick bush. An uprooted tree or shrub or a torn-off bough could become a lethal missile in this wind.

'Chad . . be careful,' she breathed. As she swung round to make a dash for the door of her bure, she heard a sound that froze her where she stood, her blood chilling in her veins. A hideously loud clanging thud, as if something solid—something metallic—had crashed into something equally solid . . . like a tree . . . or a rock-face.

'Oh, no!' The cry was torn from her. 'Chad!'

CHAPTER SEVEN

SHE started running, following the road Chad had taken up the hill, her body bent almost double against the tearing wind and the driving rain, her hair dripping wet by now, lashing across her face, half blinding her.

Dr Hayes to the rescue! With the thought came a tight ironic smile. She was recalling Chad's teasing remarks about her always wanting to leap to the rescue. If she weren't so worried, she might have laughed aloud.

She saw where the road veered off into the bush, to become little more than a rough track, and she knew it had to be the track Chad's moke had turned into. As she stumbled along, the raging wind tore through the branches of the eucalypt trees that strained over the track, a deafening, fearsome sound that reminded her that she was vulnerable too. She kept her head well down, but her eyes she kept wide open, searching, ever vigilant, as she struggled on, almost knocked off her feet by the wind, yet hardly noticing the stinging, drenching rain.

With growing apprehension and a feeling of dread, she wondered what she was going to find. She imagined herself stumbling across Chad, lying stunned, seriously injured perhaps, beside the wreck of his mini-moke; imagined herself kneeling in the mud at his side, cradling his head in her arms, assuring him in gentle, efficient tones, 'You'll be all right, Chad . . . I'm a doctor.' And she pictured him looking up at her with admiration in his eyes, whispering, 'Didn't I say that you didn't fit the fashion-model mould?'

Worried as she was, the fantasy gave her a certain piquant pleasure . . . and it did much to keep her chin up at the same time.

But as she battled on she began to feel puzzled as well as worried. Where *was* Chad? There was no sign of his moke lying crumpled against a tree or in a ditch; and certainly no sign of Chad lying injured anywhere. And yet she hadn't imagined the sound she had heard—something had definitely crashed into *something*. And she would have sworn it had happened along this very track!

But she should have found *something* by now, The sound of the crash had been so close! Surely it couldn't have come from any further along the track than this . . .

Well, she was committed now. She might as well keep on going. If nothing had happened to Chad, she would meet him on his way back, and catch a ride back to the resort with him. At least she might be able to help him *there*. There were bound to be injuries in this gale. She could still live out her fantasy . . . 'Let me help you, Chad . . . I'm a doctor too.'

But what was Chad going to say when he found her? Would he think her a crazy fool for coming after him? During a cyclone alert, for heaven's sake! After him explicitly ordering her to stay in her bure.

With the subsiding of her fears for Chad, she became more conscious of the dangers around her—of the twigs and leaves and small branches that were whipping through the air, often striking her face, her legs, her arms, leaving her skin smarting and scratched. For the first time, she gave a thought to her own saftey, and felt her first twinge of fear.

'Oh, Chad, where are you?' she cried into the wind. 'Are you on your way back yet? Are you truly all right?'

It was then that she heard a strange sound—a frightened, rending sound, from somewhere above her. As she jerked her head round, she was just in time to see a thick branch hurtling towards her.

She dodged instinctively, but not in time to avoid the branch altogether. It struck her a glancing blow on the side of the head, and she fell in a blaze of stars.

She groaned as her eyes fluttered open.

'Gemma . . . thank heaven. Lie still now . . . you're safe and sound. Just lie still and let me look at you.'

'Chad . . .?' She could see his face swimming in front of her. His lips were smiling . . . a doctor's smile, full of comfort and reassurrance. But there seemed to be more than comfort and reassurance in his eyes. She wished she knew what the look signified . . . wished she could think straighter.

'Can you remember what happened?' Chad asked as he checked out her vital signs: her pulse, her breathing, her temperature, and then peered into her eyes.

'A branch hit me—a big one. I remember ducking.'

'Good . . . good. You had a lucky escape . . . thanks to your quick thinking.'

'Where am I?' She could still hear the roar of the wind and the sound of drumming rain, but both seemed a long way away now. And she was no longer drenched to the skin, she realised. In fact she felt decidedly dry and comfortable.

'You're in my cottage. In my bed, as a matter of fact. I found you practically on my doorstep. You landed in wet grass, not mud, which was thoughtful of you. I've removed your wet clothes——'

'You've *what*?' She would have struggled upright if Chad's hand hadn't restrained her.

'Lie still, I said. Doctor's orders.' That was to remind her that he was a doctor. And doctors, he was saying, were permitted to take off their patients' clothes.

She reached up groggily and touched her head. She felt a bandage. 'Ouch!' she said. 'My head hurts.'

'It will for a while. But you haven't done too much damage.' Chad took her hand in his own, and she thought how warm it felt, and how gentle. 'You have a whopping great lump on the head and a nasty graze, but that's all. You were lucky—you didn't even need any stitches. So don't worry . . .' He gave a slight smile. 'Your looks won't be impaired—at least not for long. You'll be able to parade in public again before you know it.'

She cursed under her breath.

'What are you growling about?' Chad asked, eyeing her quizzically.

'You. You make me so mad.' She snatched back her hand.

'Well, that's gratitude for you. What have I said?'

She shut her eyes. To explain, she would have to confess the truth about her little masquerade—and that was something she felt disinclined to do. She was disappointed in him—disappointed that he still thought her main concern in life was her looks. She had hoped he might know her a little better by now . . .

And yet at the same time she knew she was being unfair. How could she really blame him, when she had quite deliberately allowed him to go on believing that she was a full-time professional model?

She sighed and opened her eyes. 'I—I'm sorry, Chad,

that I've caused you so much trouble, keeping you here, away from people who might be needing you more than I do. I'm fine now, truly, if you want to go to the resort——'

'Hush.' His finger touched her lips. 'There's no one needing me urgently at the moment. I've been in contact with Melanie and there are no serious injuries, thank God. And here's some good news for you. The cyclone has veered inland . . . we're in no danger now. The wind's dropping already.'

She closed her eyes in relief. When she opened them again, she saw that Chad was frowning at her.

'Gemma, what the hell possessed you to come after me?' He couldn't hold back the question.

It struck her then that the rescue scene she had earlier envisaged in her mind had gone sadly awry. So much for Dr Gemma Hayes, racing to the rescue! And, for that matter, so much for giving Chad a helping hand at the resort . . . working side by side with him—as a doctor. She wouldn't be much use to him now.

She winced as a knifelike pain shot through her head.

'Here . . . drink this.' Chad reached for a glass beside the bed. 'It'll help your head. Don't talk now . . . get some sleep.'

'But I want to talk,' she said contrarily. 'I'll drink it in a minute . . . when I've told you what made me come running after you. You see, I heard this terrible crash . . . I—I thought you'd hit a tree or something.'

His frown magically dissolved, and at the same time his grey eyes darkened with an emotion that for one sweet second drove away her headache completely. But all he said was, 'Ah . . . yes. I heard that too. In fact, I actually saw what happened, because it happened right in front of me. The wind picked up an empty petrol drum and slammed it into a tree.'

'But I didn't see any petrol drum.' Gemma looked puzzled.

'You wouldn't have seen it, because I picked it up and put it in the back of the moke, out of harm's way.'

'Oh.' She grimaced slightly. What a mess she had made of things! Chasing after Chad unnecessarily. Putting herself in danger. Wasting Chad's precious time having to tend to her when there must be others needing him more, despite what he'd said. So much for her foolish fantasies about coming to *his* rescue, and triumphantly announcing that she was a doctor too! So much for working alongside him at the resort . . . Dr Gemma Hayes at your service!

No point telling him she was a doctor *now*. He'd only laugh and say, 'Well, Gemma, that's too bad . . . you're going to be no help to me now—not in the condition you're in!' And she knew that it was true. She'd be no good to anybody for at least twenty-four hours.

'I'll drink that stuff now,' she said feebly, 'and get some sleep.' That was about all that she was good for.

Chad held the glass to her lips and she sipped obediently. Then she sank back against the soft pillows and closed her eyes. 'You get back to the resort,' she whispered. 'And Chad . . .' Her eyes snapped open, showing swift concern. 'Be careful, won't you?'

He smiled down at her. 'I'll be careful, Gemma. The worst is over now . . . you just get some sleep. I'll be back in an hour to check on you.'

'Thank you, Chad, for—for rescuing me,' she said drowsily, her soft lips curving into a smile. 'One rescue each . . . that makes us even.'

He kissed her suddenly on the lips.

'Why did you do that?' she whispered, startled, seeking his eyes as he drew anway.

'Because I felt like it.' He rose and stood looking down at her for a moment, a smile tipping the corners of his mouth. A heart-catchingly attractive smile, she thought as her eyelids, by now too heavy to control any more, flickered and closed.

She opened her eyes. The sun was filtering through misty blue curtains into the room. *Chad's* room, she remembered, flushing. What would Jonathan think if he could see her now, lying here in Chad's bed?

She raised herself gingerly on to one elbow. Her head didn't feel too bad . ... not too bad at all. There was barely a rustle of wind outside now, and the storm shutters had obviously been raised. Where was Chad? she wondered. Had he left for his morning surgery already? She could vaguely remember him coming in several times during the night to check on her, rousing her gently, and then, satisfied, slipping out again. As a doctor herself, she knew that he was just wanting to make sure that she hadn't slipped back into unconsciousness.

She noticed a glass of freshly squeezed orange juice beside the bed and realised that she was thirsty. She drank gratefully, and just as she was setting down the empty glass she heard footsteps.

'Good morning.'

Her eyes flicked round. Chad, looking appealingly ruffle-haired and unshaven, stood in the doorway. She swallowed—hard. He was wearing only shorts, his broad, muscular chest exposed, revealing an expanse of bronzed flesh and a tantalising V of dark hair. The sight of him brought a lump to her thoat. He looked so masculine, so strong, so—so dependable, and almost unbearably attractive. She couldn't recall ever feeling such a powerful wave of emotion when Jonathan had walked into a room . . .

And *now* what would Jonathan be thinking? she mused, the thought plucking an unbidden smile. Entertaining men in her bedroom! Correction—in *Chad's* bedroom. Oh dear . . . She bit back a giggle.

'I see you're feeling better,' Chad observed, advancing on the bed with easy grace. She felt a little breathless, as she looked up at him. She hadn't realised he was so tall . . . or that he possessed such an arresting . . . presence. A decidedly virile presence. Again she found herself comparing him with Jonathan. Why had she never had these earthy feelings about Jonathan, her fiancé? *Ex*-fiancé, she corrected herself.

'Care to share whatever is amusing you?' Chad asked pleasantly.

She hesitated, but only for a second. 'As a matter of fact, I was thinking of Jonathan,' she admitted impulsively. She knew now, if she'd had any doubts before, that she had done the right thing by breaking up with him. They had both put all the blame on her career, but that had merely been the catalyst that had brought the issue to a head. The basic, underlying truth was that she hadn't really loved him. It was as simple as that. The affection, the warmth that she had felt for him all these years had fooled her into thinking it must be the real thing. But in her deepest heart she must have known . . . Why else would she have held Jonathan at arm's length whenever he had pressurised her to sleep with him?

'Oh?' Something flickered deep in Chad's eyes 'Wishing

he was here to hold your hand?' he drawled.

She caught her breath. Now she had given Chad the wrong impression! 'No—nothing like that,' she denied swiftly. 'I was just thinking——' She stopped, suddenly unsure. What would Chad think if he knew she had been comparing him to Jonathan a moment ago—if he knew that in the comparison, he, Chad, had won hands down? Would it please him? Or would he merely laugh, and treat it as a joke? Or, worse, would he get cold feet and back away altogether, feering that she was becoming too involved? *Was* she becoming involved?

'Let's forget it,' she said hastily, wishing she'd never brought up Jonathan's name. 'He's past history now.' And I'm not thinking of getting involved with anyone else, she added under her breath. Not even with anyone as attractive as you, Dr Chad Rivers. Just as you don't want to get involved with me.

'But you still think of him,' Chad persisted, his grey eyes flat now, undreadable as stone.

'Not because I'm missing him, I assure you,' she answered, injecting lightness into her tone. That's the way, Gemma. Keep it light. Involved? You? Not on your life! You've a medical practice to think about, remember?

Chad sat down on the bed. The intimacy of the gesture—or was it simply the fact that he was so suffocatingly close?—sent a wave of heat through her body from her cheeks to her toes. And when he caught her hand and raised it to his lips, she quite stupidly seemed to lose her ability to breathe.

'Are you all right?' She realised he was frowning into her face, his grey eyes shimmering over hers like pools of liquid silver.

'I'm fine,' she said faintly. 'Just fine.'

'No headache?'

'No . . . truly, I'm fine.'

'You're a tough little cookie, aren't you?' He was kissing the tips of her fingers now, one by one. It felt deliciously sensual.

'Tough?' She felt anything but tough right now. In fact, she felt as if she could faint dead away any second.

'Well, you had a pretty nasty bump on the head. And yet here you are, as perky as a kitten. I'll take the dressing off later in the morning and have a look at your wound; I guess you're anxious to see what damage you've done to that pretty face of yours.'

She took a deep breath—partly from exasperation, partly from a sense of self-preservation. At the same time she felt a revival of her strength—and her fighting spirit.

'And why do you think I'm anxious to do that?' she asked, her eyes glinting.

'Well, you can't tell me you're not just a little bit concerned about what that tree might have done to your good looks?' He cocked a teasing eyebrow at her.

'You assured me my precious looks wouldn't be ruined,' she reminded him tartly.

'Most girls would want to make quite sure.' This was said with just a hint of his former derision, and, hearing it, she jutted out her chin.

'I've told you before—I'm not "most girls". And you'll find there are plenty of others around like me if you'd only look. Individuals, they're called, who don't leave up to—or *down* to—the stereotyped image that people like you persist in branding them with!'

'Please don't excite yourself, Gemma,' Chad begged mildly. 'You'll make your head ache. I wasn't having a shot at you . . . nor at your colleagues. I was just making an observation. And I know perfectly well that you're not like "most girls." He gave an engaging grin, trying to coax a smile from her. 'Forgive me?'

'I forgive you.' She felt a smile tugging at her lips. 'Sorry I snapped.'

He recaptured her hand and turned it over in his. 'Now, where were we?'

At once she felt breathless again; he was leading her back on to perilous ground; Chad was far easier to resist when they were sparring with each other, she decided. She tried to look unconcerned, but annoyingly she felt herself trembling. Gemma Hayes, *trembling*! And yet she couldn't seem to do anything about it.

'What's wrong?' Chad asked, the very softness of his tone doing nothing at all to calm her.

'Wrong? What could be wrong?' she challenged faintly?

'Are you asking me to read your mind?' he teased, spreading her fingers and placing her smooth palm against his cheek. Did he feel its hot clamminess? Could he also hear her heart beating a tom-tom in her chest?

She spoke severely to herself. For pity's sake, Gemma, there's no need to have the vapours just because a man is playing around with your hand. It's only your hand, for heaven's sake! Honestly, if the folks back home could only witness this tender little scene, they'd think that blow on your head had knocked all your senses—including your famed common sense—into oblivion!

She hid her musings behind a wry, 'I'm not sure I'd feel comfortable knowing that my mind was being read.'

'Ah, but you'd be surprised how often I have read your mind, Gemma, my sweet,' Chad said, his eyes glinting seductively.

'Oh?' She was momentarily startled, but she rallied quickly. Have you now, Dr Rivers? she thought smugly. You might have read my mind once or twice, but you haven't read it thoroughly. You haven't read the fact that I've been kidding you all along about what I do for a living . . . so you have quite a bit to learn about me yet, haven't you? You still think I'm a model, and you still think my looks and my figure are my primary concern in life. I still don't have your total and undivided respect *yet*!

Which she very well might have had by now, she reflected wryly, if Chad had been the one lying injured on the track, and she the one who had played the angel of mercy. But that would have been winning his respect the easy way. Was that what she wanted?

She sighed, not willing to admit that she would be prepared to accept Chad's respect now at any price, easy way out or not. So why didn't she just tell him she was a doctor and get it over with?

Because if she told him now, she would never have the satisfaction of hearing him say the words, 'I don't care if you're a model, Gemma . . . I like and respect you whatever you are.' Or even, 'I *care* for you whatever you are.' That pleasant dream aside, she had no intention of telling him while she was helplessly stuck here in bed with a bandage around her head. She had some sense of romance, after all!

The thought brought a quick smile to her lips.

'I think I'd be a wise man not to try reading your mind right now,' Chad observed ruefully. He released her hand at last, and placed it gently on the sheet. 'Feel like something to eat?' he asked, rising.

At once she was able to breathe more freely. 'Please don't worry about me, Chad. Don't you have to go to your surgery this morning? I'll get myself something when you drop me off at my bure.'

'I won't be dropping you off at your bure,' Chad said firmly. 'You'll stay right where you are until I tell you to move.'

'But I feel fine——'

'Good—but you're not fine enough yet to move from this house. You'll stay here and rest until I say you can go. If you give me the key to your bure, I'll send Melanie over to pick up some clothes for you, and anything else you want.'

Clothes! For the first time she took a quick peep under the sheet and realised she was wearing one of Chad's shirts. Her cheeks flamed. Don't get excited, you poor fool, she admonished herself hastily. He's a doctor, remember? You would have done the same for him . . .

She swallowed, trying to picture herself undressing Chad in the same circumstances. Why was it becoming so difficult lately to think like a doctor? She'd never had any trouble before.

She looked up to see Chad grinning down at her.

'You think this is a great joke, don't you?' she growled. 'Having me at your mercy.'

'What a diverting thought,' he commented, eyeing her wickedly. Then, chuckling softly, he turned on his heel and strode from the room.

She flopped back on to her pillow with a wave of relief. It was only then that she realised her head was hurting rather more than she had been prepared to admit. She closed her eyes, and in seconds, headache notwithstanding, she had drifted off to sleep.

When she opened her eyes again, there was a glass of water and a banana beside the bed, but no sign of Chad.

She ate the banana hungrily and sipped some of the water, and realised she was feeling much better.

'Oh, you're awake,' a soft voice said at the door. 'Feeling better?'

'Melanie! Yes, I am, thanks. Time I was getting up. Did you bring my clothes?'

'I did, but Chad said I wasn't to give them to you until he gets back. Strict instructions. However, I can get you something to eat. I've made a salad and thought you might like an omelette with it.'

It sounded enticing. 'Will you have one too?' Gemma asked.

'Oh—er—I've already eaten,' Melanie said, turning away. She was looking a little abstracted this morning, Gemma thought. Was it because she, Gemma, was here in Chad's house? In Chad's bed?

Whatever she felt, Melanie managed to hide it when she came back with her omelette and salad.

'I can't stay,' she apologised. 'I have to get back to the surgery. Chad just wanted me to pop in and check on you—and give you something to eat, if you wanted it. And remember, you're not to move until he gets back. It won't be long—morning surgery finishes at twelve.'

'I don't see why I can't get dressed——' Gemma began.

'Chad wants to check your wound first.' Was the girl avoiding looking directly at her, or was she imagining it? Gemma wondered as she tucked into her omelette. 'I offered to do it, but he insisted on doing it himself. He——' The girl hesitated. 'He seems rather taken with you, Gemma. I haven't seen him show as much interest as this in anyone else since I've known him.'

In anyone else but herself, did she mean? Even so, Gemma felt a tiny flare of pleasure.

'He doesn't normally get so involved with his patients,' Melanie murmured, half to herself. She had moved across to the window now and was gazing out, as if she couldn't bear to look at Gemma. Because she was in Chad's bed?

'I suppose very few of his patients fall unconscious on his doorstep,' Gemma replied wryly. 'Anyway, you can't really say he's getting involved with a *patient*. I'm more of a friend,' she said, anxious to protect Chad's professional integrity. Melanie was his nurse, after all. Could *that* be the reason the girl was a bit uptight? 'Mm . . . that was the most delicious omelette I've had for many a day,' she enthused.

For a moment Melanie didn't speak. Gemma could have sworn she saw her give a slight shiver. Was she really so upset that she was here? When at length the girl broke her silence, she still didn't turn round. 'You will be wary, won't you, Gemma?' she entreated, as if she were genuinely concerned for her. 'Chad has told me more than once that he's perfectly content living alone, and that he has no intention of getting married again. And . . .' She paused. 'Well, you know what he thinks of models.'

'Yes . . . I know.' Gemma was tempted to tell Melanie the truth, but her uncertainty about the girl's relationship with Chad held her back.

Melanie still hadn't finished. 'I have a feeling you're the kind of girl who wouldn't be satisfied with anything less than marriage.'

Gemma looked thoughtful. Whereas she, Melanie, being married herself, wouldn't have such expectations from Chad?

'There's nothing between Chad and me,' she said firmly, and felt a strange chill—almost of loss—as she uttered the words. She shook the feeling aside. 'I have my career in Sydney . . . and Chad has his life up here. I'm just here on holiday, remember?'

Melanie turned around at last. She looked pale, Gemma thought, as if she were under some kind of strain. Surely she couldn't be in *love* with Chad?

'I shouldn't be speaking to you like this.' Melanie gave a quick laugh. Now that she had made her point, Gemma speculated, did she feel she could back away? 'I—I'd better be going.' She flashed a smile at Gemma. But underneath she was plainly very tense, very edgy, for some reason—quite unlike the girl she had been a couple of days ago. What was behind it? Jealousy? Uncertainty? Apprehension? Unhappiness? Gemma examined the girl's face more closely. No . . . She wouldn't have said Melanie looked unhappy, exactly. But she certainly had *something* on her mind.

After Melanie had gone, she sank back on her pillows, and within minutes her jumbled thoughts were overtaken by sleep.

CHAPTER EIGHT

'WELL, your lump has gone down and your wound is looking good . . . no sign of infection.' Chad stood up. 'You have a shower if you like . . . but keep the water away from your wound. Then, if you feel up to it, you can get dressed.'

'Oh, I'll feel up to it,' Gemma said readily. Melanie wasn't the only one who would like to see her out of Chad's bed!

'I'll be outside. Afternoon surgery doesn't start until four,' said Chad as he left the room. 'I want to do something I've been neglecting for far too long.'

Some maintainance on the house? Gemma wondered.

But when she emerged later, freshly showered and wearing the cool shirt and wrap-around tropical skirt that Melanie had brought for her, she found Chad sitting at an easel overlooking the rocky coastline, dabbing paint on to a canvas.

He swung his head round when he heard her approaching. 'I'm pretty rusty. No rude comments. I'm just using this canvas to get my eye back in.'

She peered over his shoulder. 'You have a feel for the sea . . . there's no doubt about that.'

His glance met hers, then slid seductively from her liquid brown eyes to her soft mouth. The sun was shining into her face, burnishing her suntanned cheeks and making a golden halo of her hair.

'I wish I could paint portraits,' he said. 'I would paint you, if I could.'

She felt a flare of pleasure. 'Why, thank you, sir. Have you ever tried?'

'Yes—disastrously.' He gave a laugh—a pleasant sound, rich and throaty. 'Never again! I'll stick to seascapes. At least I have some idea of what I'm doing there . . . or what I want to do. I'm hoping it'll come back, with a bit of practice.'

'I'm glad you're painting again, Chad,' she said fervently. 'I imagine it must be awfully satisfying . . . and relaxing.'

'Therapeutic, are you trying to say?' He smiled again, without strain. 'Yes, I can't deny it. But it can be frustrating too, when it doesn't turn out the way you would like.'

She looked criticaly at the canvas. 'For someone who hasn't painted for a while, you should be quite pleased. And it can only improve with practice. Anyway, are you painting just for your own pleasure and satisfaction, or do you intend exhibiting and selling your paintings one day?'

'Hell, no. It's just a hobby. I wouldn't even thrust them on my friends. It's like sailing. Sheer self-indulgence. Do *you* have any particular hobbies—apart from water sports and reading romantic novels?'

She shot him a quick look to see if he was having a shot at her, but his expression was teasingly warm and friendly, free of his former cynicism.

'I don't have all that much spare time for hobbies,' she admitted at length. 'Sometimes I manage to get to a play or a concert, and I have quite a collection of classical records I often play while I'm——' she nearly said 'studying', but changed it hastily to, 'home of an evening.

But during the day or at weekends, if I'm free, I like to head for the water. That's where I find *my* relaxation.'

He nodded. 'Yes . . . it has a lure all right—the sea. I think I'd have gone mad at times if I hadn't been able to go sailing. There's nothing more relaxing. This——' he indicated the canvas with a wave of his brush '—is just cream on the cake.'

'Then you're happy here, Chad,' she heard herself asking, 'living on your own?'

He looked up at her, his glance bemused. 'Happy? I don't know that I'd call it "happy", exactly. But I've been moderately content, I guess. Being out of the rat-race—and being on my own—has certainly given me time to think.' He gave a sloping grin. 'That's something I never bothered to do much of in the past. I guess I never made time for it. It does you good to look at your life once in a while, to weigh up your values . . . ponder your mistakes . . . and take a good hard look at your priorities. You see things a whole lot more clearly.'

Gemma bit her lip. 'You sound as if you have . . . regrets about something, Chad. Are you talking about your—your marriage? Do you mean you have regrets about not spending more time with your wife?'

He laid down his brush and took her hand. 'Let's go for a walk,' he said. 'Do you feel up to it? It's rather pleasant along the clifftop.'

She nodded, swallowing, wondering if he was about to unburden himself at last. Or was this an attempt to change the subject?

They followed a narrow, overgrown path that meandered through the bush, close to the cliff edge, picking their way over twigs and branches that had been torn off by the wind, and brushing aside drops of water that splashed on to their faces from the trees above. The air was hot and steamy after the rain, and the tropical undergrowth had a fresh green lushness.

'You were asking about my marriage,' Chad said eventually. She had to strain to hear him over the raucous din of the cockatoos. 'You're right, Gemma . . . about the regrets. Nobody likes to admit failure.'

'You're saying your marriage was a—a mistake?' Gemma asked as five brilliantly coloured parrots, in a blur of red and green, took flight at their approach, and circled in confusion.

'Let's just say . . . we didn't have enough in common.' Chad pushed aside a low-hanging vine that was clinging to the branch of a she-oak tree. 'It didn't seem important at first. When you're both busy, wrapped up in your work, you make very few demands on each other, and you think that the little time you do spend together is enough. You think of it as special and precious . . . and so it was, for a while. But whatever we had didn't last; it had no solid base. Perhaps, if it had . . .' He broke off with a shrug of regret. 'Looking back, I see now that neither of us was prepared to make a total commitment. We never really shared our lives, our inner selves. We were both too selfish to make the effort.'

'But if you had truly loved each other . . .' Gemma's teeth tugged at her lip. Chad didn't strike her as the kind of man who would marry without love.

'There's a fine line,' Chad said drily, 'between "true love" and——' He paused, shrugging. 'And infatuation . . . fascination . . . whatever it was in our case. It didn't last because it had no depth. I don't think either of us knew the real meaning of the word "love" when we blithely hurtled into marriage.'

And have you discovered the real meaning since, Chad? Gemma wondered, her breath catching in her throat. Did you discover it, perhaps, with the married Melanie—and are you trying to repress that forbidden love by seeing me instead? And what do you feel for me, Chad? Anything at all—beyond a casual liking and a glimmer of admiration?

But she asked none of these questions aloud, and Chad went on talking, still in the same dry, musing tone, about his marriage to Roxanne.

'After only a few months we'd started to grow apart . . . we were both content to go our own way, do our own thing.'

'How did you meet in the first place?' Gemma asked curiously, her gaze momentarily diverted by a row of fruit bats hanging from a low branch. Their wings, she thought, were like velvet. Gossamer wings.

'At an art exhibition,' Chad told her, his mouth twisting with self-irony. 'I had started dabbling in a bit of painting in my spare time, and Roxanne offered to give me some lessons . . . privately.' His shoulders lifted and fell. 'Even that failed to provide a lasting bond between us. She was so much more involved, more intense about the subject than I was. I didn't have the time—or the same dedication, I guess. To me, art was just a form of recreation—something to enjoy in snatched moments. Not something serious to dissect and agonise over. Even our friends provided no common ground—I couldn't take to the arty crowd she mixed with and she found my friends stuffy—and any medical talk depressed her.' He gave a short laugh, with a touch of irony. 'And she loathed sport of any kind—sailing most of all.'

Gemma's sense of humour brought a faint gleam to her eyes. 'You were both labouring against extreme odds,' she said gravely.

Chad tilted his head at her, his own eyes glinting with a responsive light. But there was a sigh in his voice as he muttered, 'Perhaps, if I'd tried a bit harder . . . if I hadn't been so caught up in my work . . . if I'd given a bit more of myself . . . Perhaps, damn it, if we'd taken the time to have children . . .'

'You would have liked children, Chad?'

'Not then. But now . . .' He shrugged, frowning into the mid-distance, straight through a curtain of vines draped across their path. It was Gemma who leapt forward this time to brush them aside. 'Children need a lot of loving . . . a lot of time,' Chad said grimly. 'I'd be prepared to give that love and that time now, if I had the chance again. But poor Roxanne will never have that chance . . .' A muscle clenched along his jaw. 'She's gone. A beautiful, young, healthy, talented woman . . . gone—just like that!' He clicked his fingers. 'Within minutes. And I wasn't even with her.'

'And you've been feeling angry and guilty and sorry for yourself ever since.' Without meaning to, Gemma spoke her thoughts aloud. But, now that she had, she decided it might as well be in for a penny, in for a pound. 'Isn't it time you stopped punishing yourself, Chad? Roxanne has found her peace. Isn't it about time you found yours?'

She sounded like a psychoanalyst! All she needed was a couch! The thought brought self-mocking laughter to her lips. 'Just listen to me! I'm afraid I have this bad habit of never minding my own business. It's because I—I care about people, not because I want to pry,' she assured him.

And I care about you especially, Dr Rivers, she realised with a mild sense of shock. Chad had suffered more than the loss of his wife. On top of his natural grief, he had suffered a sense of failure, a sense of guilt, of remorse. Had talking about it helped him at all? she wondered. 'He seldom mentions his wife,' Melanie had said once. Perhaps now that he had, now that he had talked openly about his marriage, and bared his soul, he could lay Roxanne to rest.

She felt Chad's arm slide round her waist. 'We'd better head back . . . I want you to rest,' was all he said, but the expression in his eyes and the pressure of his fingers said far more.

They didn't speak for some time after that; Gemma sensed a new rapport between them which made it unnecessary. Up in the branches, the birds twittered and shrilled and cackled in a deafening chorus, and the sweet fragrance of frangipani wafted in the humid air.

This is a beautiful place, she thought dreamily, letting her gaze drift around. Beyond the cliff edge, the water sparkled like liquid silver, and a flock of silver gulls wheeled high in the pale blue sky. A beautiful retreat from the world . . .

Chad had come here, she saw quite clearly now, not only to set up a sorely needed medical service and to do his research on marine stingers—though naturally they would have been an important and vital part of it. But there had been more complex reasons besides: the need to atone for his feelings of guilt and failure . . . the need for time and solitude to look more closely at himself and his way of life, to reassess his values and ideals, and work out where his priorities really lay . . .

Was he close to finding his answers? she wondered pensively, glancing up covertly under cover of her thick lashes to examine his face. As her eyes traced the line of his ruggedly attractive profile, taking in the strong line of his jaw, the firm, sensual mouth, the way his tanned skin was pulled taut over his cheekbones, she felt a wave of light-headedness sweep over her, and she might have spun to the ground if Chad's arm hadn't been supporting her.

'Gemma, what's wrong?' His grip tightened. 'Here, let me carry you.' Before she could protest, he had swept her into his arms as if she were no more weighty than a feather. 'A fine doctor I am, keeping you out in this heat.'

Cradled against his chest, she felt close to swooning again. And yet she would have sworn if wasn't the heat or even the knock on her head that was affecting her. She couldn't understand it. She had never been on the verge of fainting before, not even last year, when she had been struck down with a virulent bout of the 'flu, not even when she had witnessed her first operation. The only previous time she had felt the least bit light-headed was when Chad had walked into his bedroom earlier today and had sat down beside her on the bed. But that had been nothing like this . . . This had been more of a shock-reaction. The shock of sudden awareness, the shock of realising——

Dear heaven, she thought, with dizzying comprehension, I love this man! It hit her with the power of a thunderbolt. And then her common sense argued, but it doesn't happen this way. It can't! Adolescents might fall in love in this highly unlikely sentimental fashion, but not a grown woman of twenty-five, a down-to-earth doctor, a self-assured woman with a broken engagement still fresh and raw behind her!

She stared at the buttons on his shirt as she tried to pull herself together, to regain her equilibrium. Maybe, when she had completely recovered from her blow on the head, the feeling would pass. Being so sudden, how could it be relied on to be genuine? How could it last?

A tiny voice taunted, What you felt for Jonathan didn't last . . . so what does suddenness have to do with it? No . . . An unconscious smile curved her lips. This was different—wonderfully, excitingly different. Deep down inside, she knew this wasn't a feeling that was going to pass . . . It had been growing, bit by bit, almost from the moment she had met him. That explosive awareness a moment ago had only been her own subconscious letting her know the truth . . .

'That is a very sweet and very tantalising smile.' Chad's smouldering gaze drank in her soft lips. 'I daren't ask what it means.' He smiled then, too, a smile of such tenderness that it tore at her heart.

And I daren't tell you, she mused with a hidden sigh. It's far too soon. You're only just getting to know me. And if you have any sense at all, Gemma Hayes, you will realise that you are only just getting to know him! You'd be mad to rush things and risk . . .

She closed her eyes, wanting to hide them from Chad, for fear he would read what was in them. Oh, Chad, she thought, I don't want to lose you!

With a twinge, she recalled what Melanie had said the other day, about Chad swearing that he would never marry again. Having failed once, she could understand him being wary of risking a serious involvement, and especially marriage, a second time. But supposing he fell in love, too—genuinely in love this time. Would he change his mind? And what if he did? What about her career, the partnership she had been offered in Sydney?

She lolled back in Chad's arms as a wave of tiredness swept over her. She didn't feel up to thinking about any of that just now . . . Maybe that knock on the head was the real cause after all of all this heightened emotion!

When Chad's small green weatherboard cottage came into view, he carried her straight inside without even pausing to pick up his easel and paints on the way and, despite her protests, deposited her firmly on his bed.

'Now . . . about time the doctor checked you over.'

She took a long, deep breath to calm herself, quite sure he was going to find her pulse-rate riotously fast, her breathing erratic, and her temperature soaring, but he made no comment as he finished his examination and stood up. 'I suggest you have a nap while I go to the surgery. I'll only be gone a couple of hours. Will you be all right?'

'Chad, I'm not staying here in your——' A swift finger silenced her in mid-sentence.

'You'll stay right there until I tell you otherwise. We'll discuss it when I get back. I'll send Melanie to check on you in an hour's time. No arguments.' He was gone before she could protest.

How would Melanie like that? she pondered, sinking back against the pillows. Then she must have fallen asleep, because the next thing she knew, Melanie was bending over her.

'Feeling all right?' she asked, and Gemma nodded as she pulled herself upright. She did feel good, she realised. Not even a trace of a headache. Of her heartache, she wasn't so sure.

Melanie, she was relieved to see, was looking less tense than she had been earlier in the day, and she showed no sign this time of wanting to avoid looking at her in Chad's bed. Of course, I'm not really *in* it this time, Gemma rationalised. I'm lying on top of it, fully dressed.

'Anything you want?' Melanie asked with a smile. 'I've brought you some lemonade.' She indicated a bottle and glass beside the bed.

'Thanks, Melanie . . . no, there's nothing else I want. I'm quite capable of getting it if I do. Chad's making an awful fuss of a simple concussion. I'm perfectly all right now.' My head is, at any rate, she reflected wryly. I can't say as much for my heart.

'He's being wise to keep an eye on you,' Melanie said briskly. 'After all, you are here on the island alone. If you'd had someone staying with you, it would have been different.'

Chad would never have taken her under his wing? Was that what she was saying? Gemma felt a faint dip in her spirits. Was that the only reason Chad had been so attentive—because he felt responsible for her?

'Well, I must get back to the surgery,' Melanie said. 'Chad just wanted me to look in on you—and he asked me to bring in his easel and paints. It's great news that he's painting again, isn't it?'

'Yes, it's wonderful,' Gemma agreed. 'Melanie, don't worry about bringing in the paints—I can bring them in myself. I'm not staying here all day.' She swung her legs over the side of the bed as she spoke.

Melanie looked startled. 'You're to stay right there! Chad's orders. And I've already brought in the paints—that is, I've put them in the old iron shed outside—his "studio", Chad quaintly called it. Good to see he can joke about a subject he's been avoiding for so long . . .' She flashed Gemma a smile. 'Must fly . . . be good.'

'Thanks for coming, Melanie. Bye!' Gemma called after her. Despite Chad's orders, she left the bed and took her lemonade into the adjoining lounge-dining-room, which, she realised, after poking her head through a couple of doorways, was the only other real room in the house. As she sank into a rather lumpy two-seater settee, she wondered where Chad had slept last night. This settee wouldn't have been anywhere long enough for his rangy frame, and there were no other bedrooms—only a tiny kitchen and a bathroom which doubled as a laundry. Surely he hadn't slept on the floor?

Well, that does it, she decided. I'm going back to my *bure* tonight, whether he gives me permission or not!

Her gaze roved idly around the room as she sipped her lemonade. Like the rest of the little timber cottages, the room was small and functional, possessing only the barest necessities—a table, a couple of upright chairs, the couch she was sitting on, and a handsome leather armchair, which looked rather incongruous beside the other, rather cheap-looking furniture. Had Chad brought it from his original home? There was a large ceiling fan—no air-conditioning here! Rough matting covered the bare boards, and the walls were painted a pale blue-green, the colour of the sea. In a way, the place was more like a weekend beach shack than a permanent home. But then, Chad was only renting the place, and he had never intimated that he was going to stay on the island permanently. In fact, now that he had finished researching his treatise on marine stingers, and achieved what he had set out to do on the island, would he start thinking of his own life, of moving on, of seeking new challenges?

How she would love to seek those new challenges with him!

You're not forgetting that Sydney offer, are you, Gemma? her conscience reminded her. She bit her lip guiltily. Her life back home in Sydney seemed so hazy, so remote at this moment. All she wanted to think about was

Chad! With a sigh, she stood up and started wandering around the room, hoping to get to know Chad better by seeing and feeling and touching the things that he saw and felt and touched . . .

Didn't he ever have his family or his friends from the mainland to stay, or to visit? Apparently not—there wouldn't be room! If he did have visitors, presumably they stayed at the resort and he entertained them there. Somehow, she had the feeling he hadn't had too many visitors in the past two or so years. He gave the impression that he had cut himself off entirely from his past life. Even from his own family? He had never mentioned his family, she realised now. Did he have parents? Brothers and sisters?

There were a couple of maritime prints on the walls, and one original painting, a tropical landscape which brought to vivid life the lush Queensland rain forest it depicted. It was signed 'Roxanne Wilson'.

Wilson must have been Roxanne's maiden name, Gemma mused. As she stood back to admire the painting, she wondered idly if Chad's wife had ever called herself Roxanne Rivers in her private life. From what Chad had told her about Roxanne, and about their marriage, it didn't seem likely. The two had lived largely separate, independent existences, with little or nothing in common, both wrapped up in their own separate careers. They had even had their own separate friends.

She went on gazing at the painting, but she was looking inwards now, at the parallel of her own engagement to Jonathan. If they had gone ahead and married, would she have ended up like Roxanne: a woman more committed to her career than her marriage? Would they have drifted apart in the end, the way Roxanne and Chad had?

Jonathan must have seen the danger lying ahead, to put his ultimatum to her in the first place. You have a choice. Me . . . or a full-time career . . .

I did him a favour, Gemma thought, by letting him go. For a marriage and a full-time career to work successfully, you need a rock-solid love. You have to be willing to make compromises, sacrifices; you have to really work at it. I wasn't prepared to make any compromises for Jonathan. Because I never loved him enough . . .

The sound of Chad's mini-moke disturbed her reverie, bringing her back to earth with a start. Heavens, had an hour gone by already?

She went to meet him at the door, flushing slightly as the thought flitted through her mind that to anyone secretly watching—thankfully that was unlikely out here in the bush—she must look the part of the devoted little wife, welcoming her husband home from work. She had never seen herself in that role before! The thought drew a tiny smile.

'Well, you look a hundred per cent better . . .' Chad grasped her shoulders with his strong, gentle fingers and devoured her flushed face with such a burning intensity in his grey eyes that she felt her body would melt and float away. 'You have colour back in your cheeks and a new spring in your step. Do you feel as good as you look?'

She had time to gulp before she could answer. 'Better. And it's high time I got out of your hair . . .'

He crinkled his brow, making a comical attempt to look up at his unruly dark hair. 'I don't feel as if you're in my hair at all,' he quipped, and as he spoke he pulled her closer, folding her in his arms. 'It feels good to have someone to come home to,' he said, brushing her silky hair with his lips.

It felt so right, so comfortable in his arms. And yet at the same time she felt a momentary qualm. If Chad ever married again, he would want a full-time wife next time, not another full-time career-wife. Even if he came to care for her the way she cared for him, even if it grew into the greatest love in the world, she still couldn't see Chad wanting a full-time working wife . . . he wouldn't want to risk making the same mistake a second time. Risking *failure* a second time.

For you, Chad, I would work part-time, she vowed in swift desperation. I would give up working altogether! I would give up the Sydney partnership, move away from my family, my home, do anything for you. Because I love you as I've never loved any man before!

She didn't realise she was clinging to him until he drew back a little. Gently, he slid his hand from her shoulder and brought it up to cup her chin. He peered intently into her face.

She quickly masked her features. What was she thinking of? Was she mad? Fantasising about being married to Chad! Just because he had made a flippant remark about her meeting him at the door. Heaven help her if Chad had been reading her mind this time. He'd probably run a mile!

'I really must be going,' she said, but, as she tried to free herself, Chad's grip tightened.

'You are going nowhere, young lady. We're going to sit down and have a cool drink together, and then I'm going to cook dinner. For both of us.'

She was momentarily diverted. 'You can cook, Chad?'

'Don't look so surprised. I've been looking after myself for a good while now. I don't always eat out, you know. I suppose you cook superbly—as you do everything else?'

He tilted his head at her.

'Afraid not. I'm a lousy cook,' she admitted. The truth was, she hadn't had the time to learn. She had worked such long hours at the hospital, and the staff canteen had provided such cheap, nutritious meals, that she hadn't bothered, hadn't found it necessary.

Glancing up at him, she saw his lip tilt mockingly. 'Too mundane a job for a high-class fashion model?' he taunted.

She felt swift dismay wash over her. Didn't he know her well enough by now to know that she would be prepared to have a go at anything; that to her, no task would be too 'mundane' to attempt, that she considered nothing to be 'beneath' her? And yet, to be fair, how could she expect Chad to know her as well as that in only a few days—especially when she had been deliberately deceiving him about her true profession? But, even with that in mind, she still couldn't stifle her disappointment.

'Why the frown?' Chad looked puzzled. 'I was only teasing. It doesn't matter that you can't cook—as long as *I* can.'

'It's not that,' she mumbled, in a voice that was even more muffled now because he had gathered her close to him again and her face was half-buried in his shirt. 'It's just that you implied——' She broke off impatiently, demanding with new resolution, 'Chad, why are you so bitter about models? What do you have against them?'

'Bitter?' She sensed his withdrawal. 'I'm not bitter about *you* . . . and that's all that counts. Isn't it?'

She swallowed. 'No, it isn't. Not really. I don't like to see you bitter at all, Chad . . . because it spills over on to other people who I'm sure don't deserve it. I'm not thinking of myself . . . I'm thinking of—of other models.

Models in general. They're not all selfish and egotistical and useless at everything but beautifying themselves.' She realised she was speaking from limited first-hand experience, though from what she had observed of Zara Magatelli's models the other day she felt confident that underneath all the greasepaint and the teased hairdos and the frantic scramble to look just right for their public, models were not much different from herself or anyone else.

Chad didn't answer for a long moment. Then, finally, he nodded, though a lingering bitterness was still evident in his eyes. 'OK, so I have scars,' he admitted with a shrug, adding, with the ghost of a grin, 'I've lived with them a long time . . .'

'Won't you tell me about it, Chad?' she urged softly.

She watched the play of emotions on his face, and then he seemed to make up his mind. Releasing her gently, he motioned to her to sit down. 'I'll get that drink. What will you have? Fruit juice? Lemonade? Or something stronger?'

'I've drunk all your lemonade,' she confessed. 'Fruit juice will do nicely, thanks.' She smiled in an attempt to hide a feeling of apprehension. Just how deep and lasting were these scars Chad had referred to? Were they going to go on eating away at him forever?

When they were seated side by side on the settee, with Chad's arm draped along the back, and the tips of his fingers lightly brushing the nape of her neck, sending shivery impulses down her spine, he finally broke his silence.

'My mother was a model,' he told her in a voice devoid of any emotion. 'A top photographic model—she was in demand all over the world. She had the looks for it . . .'

For a second, Chad's gaze rested, broodingly, on Gemma's face. 'My father pursued her relentlessly until she agreed to marry him—on condition that she could continue with her modelling and her jet-setting life-style. She didn't need to work—my father was extremely well-heeled in his own right—a financial wizard. But modelling was in my mother's blood. She only gave it up long enough to have me—the son my father wanted. And then she went back to what she loved the most.'

Hearing the cynicism in his voice, Gemma couldn't resist asking, 'You don't think a married woman should have a full-time career, Chad?' She swallowed before adding, 'And yet you married a career-woman yourself . . .'

'That was different,' Chad said tightly. 'We both agreed beforehand that we wouldn't have any children . . .'

'Because you suffered yourself as a child?' Gemma probed gently.

'As an infant, a child, a youth . . .' Chad's mocking tone couldn't completely erase the pain and the resentment that obviously still ran deep. 'I rarely saw my mother . . . or my father either, for that matter. He always insisted on travelling with her. He used his overseas business interests as an excuse. I was left with a succession of nannies, aunts, friends, grandparents—whoever would have me.'

His fingers had somehow become entangled in Gemma's hair, and he was coiling a strand of it around and around the tip of one of them as he spoke.

'I spent half my life in boarding schools,' he muttered. 'Even during the school holidays, my parents were seldom around—which meant being shunted off again to relatives and friends.'

'Ouch!' said Gemma, her head jerking round suddenly.

'Did I pull your hair? Sorry.' He released the strand of hair he had unwittingly almost tugged from her head, and tenderly caressed the nape of her neck. 'I wasn't always unhappy, don't get me wrong . . . but I swore when I grew up that I'd never inflict that kind of life on to any child of mine. No prizes for guessing why I took my bitterness out on the modelling profession . . .'

'And what about your father?' Gemma asked. 'How did you feel about him?'

Chad shrugged. 'I suppose you see me as a typical male chauvinist for directing all my bitterness at my mother. Perhaps it was because as a small child I felt I needed my mother more. Or perhaps I loved her more . . . I don't know. I'm afraid I disappointed my father, because I didn't share his passion for money. He lived it and breathed it—and worked hard at it. You could say that while his goddess was my mother, his god was money. He made it hand over fist—he couldn't seem to go wrong. My mother was earning a top model's salary at the same time. No one in our family ever went without the material things of life,' he added drily.

'You've been speaking in the past tense, Chad . . .' Gemma looked at him questioningly.

'My father died about five years ago,' Chad said tonelessly. 'My mother has survived his loss admirably—she's even remarried.' He withdrew his hand at last. 'Let's leave the rest until later . . . I have some fresh barramundi in the fridge that I brought home at lunch-time. How about grilled fish for dinner with stir-fried vegetables?'

'Sounds wonderful,' she said, springing to her feet. 'Let me help.'

CHAPTER NINE

'DO YOU ever see your mother, Chad?' Gemma asked. She had deliberately waited until they had finished Chad's superbly cooked meal before reintroducing the subject of his family. Chad had made some coffee, and they were back on the settee, this time sitting sedately at either end.

'Not if I can help it,' Chad said indifferently.

'But you do see her occasionally?' Gemma pressed. It worried her that Chad still harboured this resentment against his mother. It had all happened so long ago!

'Occasionally. At weddings and funerals.'

Gemma took a deep breath. 'So you do still speak to each other . . . Well, that's a start,' she said with the hint of a smile. 'Chad——' She hesitated.

'I won't bite,' he encouraged, his expression relaxing slightly.

'Chad, can't you bury the past and become friends?' she pleaded. 'If you don't, one day you'll be attending another funeral—your mother's,' she said brutally, 'and by then it will be too late.'

The ceiling fan whirring overhead was the only sound in the room. Dusk had long since fallen, and a shaded lamp threw dark shadows across Chad's taut face. She appealed to him. 'I've come to know you as a compassionate man, Chad. The fact that you chose medicine when you could have followed in your father's footsteps shows that you care more about people than material things. I can't imagine that you don't have some feeling for your mother. If you only gave her a chance—if you could bring yourself to meet her half-way—I'm sure you would find that she cares for you too, and that she's very proud of you as well. As for this grudge you have against models, Chad—well, it seems a rather baseless grudge to me.'

'Oh, yes?' His eyes glinted. 'Well, I can understand your wanting to stick up for the modelling fraternity.'

'It's not that, Chad, as you will——' She clamped her lips shut, biting the rest off. She had a little more to say before she made any confessions of her own. 'From what you've told me about your parents, Chad, they would have travelled the world regardless—even if your mother hadn't been a model. Your father had overseas business interests, you said, that would have taken him away—and if he was as devoted to your mother as you say, he would have wanted her to go with him.'

Chad looked down into her intense face and the harsh lines etched into his cheeks softened. He put his empty cup down, took hers from her and put that down too, then, shifting closer, pulled her into his arms so that her head was nestled comfortably in the curve of his shoulder. She could feel the corded muscles of his chest through the silky fabric of his shirt, feel the heat rising from his skin, hear his heartbeat throbbing against her ear.

The vibration of his voice, when he spoke, seemed to roll through her from her head to her toes. 'I know what you're trying to do,' he said, sounding amused and tender at the same time. 'You're trying to convince me that all models aren't selfish, callous creatures who turn into selfish, callous mothers . . .'

She glanced up at him and found him still gazing into her face. There was something in his expression now that filled her with mingled anticipation and wonder—and guilt! Chad still thought she was a model—and yet he was looking at her as if—talking about 'mothers' as if——

'Chad——' she began, a note of appeal in her voice. The time had come to tell him the truth. It would be pointless now to keep up the pretence any longer. Chad no longer cared that she was a model—he liked her anyway. Perhaps more than liked, came the wistful hope. It was a pity in a way, she reflected with a poignant half-smile, that her fantasies were not going to come true after all—those romantic fantasies in which she saw herself rescuing Chad from the jaws of death, or rushing to help him at the scene of some catastrophic disaster, and announcing triumphantly that she was a doctor . . .

Ah, well, it couldn't be helped. There really could be no more romantic setting than this, she decided dreamily . . . snuggled up against Chad on his couch, with his warm breath fanning her cheek and her head fitting so perfectly into the hollow of his shoulder . . .

And alone . . . quite alone.

'Chad, I—I haven't been quite honest with you.' Damn, she thought. That's not the way I meant to start! It sounds as if I have something to be ashamed of! And I'm *not* ashamed . . . I had a perfectly valid reason for letting Chad go on thinking I was a model. He'll understand when I explain . . . he must!

When she felt him stiffen, her confidence faltered—until she heard him ask laconically, 'You've realised you love Jonathan after all?'

She felt a tiny thrill that Chad's first concern should be

to know whether she still had any feeling for Jonathan. Could it mean that he genuinely cared for her?

'Chad, it's nothing to do with Jonathan,' she assured him vehemently, struggling to sit up, anxious to face him eye to eye. Anxious to explain. 'It—it's about the kind of work I do.'

'Work?' His hand had strayed to her hair. 'Who wants to talk about work? If that's all it's about, it can wait.'

She felt a flare of surprised relief. He didn't care what she did for a living. He cared for her anyway. Even so, she wanted to get it off her chest . . . She wanted no more secrets between them.

'Chad, we should talk about it now before——'

'Before what?' Now his fingers were trailng down her cheek, along the line of her throat, and she could feel her limbs—and her mind—turning to water at his touch. 'Later,' he murmured.

'But Chad——' she protested weakly. She got no further; Chad had brought his hand up and was pressing a finger to her lips.

'If you don't stop chattering,' he warned, looking down at her in mock censure, 'I'll be forced to put you over my knee and spank you.'

She uttered a sigh and sank back in his arms. 'I'd rather you put me over your knee and kissed me,' she invited, her dark eyes boldly challenging.

She saw something flicker far back in his eyes. His hand was on her cheek now, his fingertips lightly brushing her skin. 'You issued a similar invitation once before,' he reminded her softly. His face was tantalisingly close to hers but, frustratingly, he made no attempt to kiss her. 'Then you backed away, insisting you were only kidding.'

'I'm not kidding now,' she assured him. I'm all yours, she added under her breath. I've lost my pride, my self-control, my doubts, and my heart. I love you, Chad Rivers, and I'm going to make you love me. I'm going to fight for you as I've never fought—never wanted to fight—for any man before in my life . . .

'And you really want me to kiss you?' Chad taunted softly, sliding his hand down to curl his fingers under her chin.

The devil! He was trying to make her beg!

'You want me to beg, I'll beg,' she muttered through her teeth. She gazed up into his face, letting the love she felt for him blaze from her eyes. 'Kiss me, Chad,' she said huskily, reaching up to stroke his cheek. 'I'm begging . . .'

Chad appeared to catch his breath. 'You're a she-devil,' he breathed. 'A man would have to be made of stone to resist an appeal like that from you . . .' Almost before he had finished speaking, he was crushing her to him, his mouth devouring hers in a wild, bruising kiss that sent throbbing whirls of intense pleasure spiralling through her.

Her mouth opened of its own accord beneath the hard pressure of his, her senses reeling as his tongue flicked over her swollen lips, before thrusting deep inside to taste the sweet warmth of her mouth. A low moan rose from her throat, and with a choking sound Chad gathered her in his arms and, with his mouth still firmly locked to hers, carried her effortlessly to his bedroom. There, with only the pearly light of the moon to guide him, he eased her down on to his bed, and lowered himself down beside her.

Their bodies were still entwined, Chad's mouth still hungrily in possession of hers, his hands moving over her body, exploring the soft lines of her back, her waist, her hips. Of their own volition her arms crept around his neck, her fingers twisting in the soft curls at his nape.

Finally Chad tore his mouth away to mutter thickly, 'Gemma, Gemma, is it true? Have I really found you at last?'

She blinked up at him, her eyes dark and liquid, her mouth still burning from his kiss. 'Found me?' she echoed, her throat constricting with hope and longing.

'Are you the woman I've been looking for all my life?'

Her heart went into a spin. Still breathless, she managed to caution herself. Now don't get carried away, Gemma. If he's asking questions, it means he can't be sure yet. He's made one big mistake in his life—he'll want to be very sure of himself, and of you, before he commits himself a second time. So take it nice and slow . . . a step at a time.

She looked up at him from under her sweeping lashes. 'Are you the man I've been looking for all mine?' she countered, her tone husky, gently teasing.

Something flashed between them, more telling than words. But, when Chad finally spoke, it was to ponder his own question, not hers. 'I could be wrong . . .' Now his voice too was teasing. 'You're inclined to be stubborn . . . impetuous . . . even foolhardy on occasion . . . and at times you can be aggravatingly independent. Ah, but what the sight and smell and the feel of you do to me!' He was unbuttoning her blouse as he spoke, his fingers fiery hot on her skin as he peeled the soft fabric aside. When he discovered she was wearing no bra, he made a husky sound low in his throat, and traced a burning path down her throat with his lips, giving a tormented groan as his mouth reached the creamy flesh of her exposed breast.

Instinctively, her body arched against him, her nipples

throbbing, hardening under his touch, her body vibrating
with a liquid fire. Passion, love, desire, flowed through her
like warm honey, her response heightened by the words
she had just heard. 'Chad, Chad,' she whispered helplessly
as his lips and his tongue played with the rosy peak of her
breast. She clung to him, her breath coming in long,
surrendering moans, wanting to cry out 'More, more!'
where before, with Jonathan, she would have been crying
out 'Stop, stop!'

Suddenly her hands were ripping at the buttons of his
shirt. She longed to feel closer to him; longed to press her
hot, naked breast to his, to feel the rough texture of his
bare skin against her smooth softness. She wanted the heat
of their bodies to fuse, to ignite both of them to searing
heights of passion that neither of them had ever reached
before.

As her fingers clawed at his shirt, she realised dimly that
Chad was drawing back, reaching out to flick on the lamp
beside the bed, and his expression as he looked down at
her filled her with dismay. He looked apologetic! More
than apologetic—*contrite*.

To cover the swift hurt that leapt inside her, she took
refuge in banter.

'Tell me you were only kidding and you're a dead man,'
she quipped, her eyes threatening him. Her voice was a
trifle breathless, but what did he expect after what he had
been doing to her a moment ago?

'Oh, I wasn't kidding. Far from it. But I remembered in
time that I happen to be a doctor—*your* doctor while
you're here in my care.' He tweaked her chidingly under
the chin. 'You're still my patient . . . and I don't play
around with my patients, no matter how delectable or how
willing they may be.'

'Chad, I may have been a patient of yours when you dragged me in——' she began, struggling to sit up.

'Carried,' Chad corrected. 'I carried you in. As if you were rare china.'

'When you carried me in, then. But I'm better now, and——'

'You're still in my care. You're still my patient. You've had a nasty knock on the head, and when you have concussion you need watching for a day or two. For goodness' sake, Gemma, cover yourself up—I may be a doctor, but I'm only human.'

'And I may be your patient, but *I'm* only human,' she retorted archly. She yanked at her shirt. 'There! Is that better, *Doctor*?' She thrust out her chin. 'And in case you don't know it, Dr Rivers, "a day or two" is already up. I'm better now, and I want you to take me back to my bure . . . right now.' Where I'll no longer be your patient, she thought, a wicked gleam leaping to her eye.

'You can go back tomorrow,' Chad said firmly, rolling off the bed. He stood over her, smiling a crookedly rueful smile, his stance emphasising the force of his thighs, the leanness of his hips, his rangy frame exuding an animal magnetism that left her weak with longing. 'I'll take you back on my way to the surgery in the morning. You're staying here overnight. Right here in this bed. *Alone* in this bed.' He appeared to grit his teeth as he uttered the word 'alone'.

'And where do you think you're going to sleep?' she demanded. 'Where did you sleep last night?'

'I slept right outside your door. Where I'll sleep again tonight. On the camp stretcher.'

'I didn't see any camp stretcher.'

'No, because I have tidy habits and I folded it up and
put it away in a cupboard.'

'Then you didn't sleep on the floor?'

He gave a snort of laughter. 'Is that what you thought?
No, I didn't sleep on the floor. But maybe I should
tonight. Thinking about how uncomfortable I am might
keep my mind off you.'

Her pulse quickened. 'You don't have to sleep on the
floor, Chad—or on the camp stretcher. You could watch
me much more closely here in your own bed—right beside
me.'

'You witch! And to think that out there on the boat the
other day you fooled me into thinking you weren't that
kind of girl.'

'I never was that kind of girl—until I met you.'

He eyed her speculatively. 'Aren't you forgetting
Jonathan—your fiancé?'

'*Ex*-fiancé. And I never—we never——' She faltered,
heat stealing into her cheeks. Damn you, Chad Rivers, she
thought. I'm telling you things I've never told anyone
before . . . just as a moment ago I was *doing* things,
wanting things I've never done or wanted before . . . hard-
nosed, down-to-earth doctor though I am. But then, I've
never loved anyone like this before, with all my heart and
soul and—her colour deepened—all my body too.

It scared her a bit. 'He'll never marry you,' Melanie
had told her once. And he had yet to tell her he loved
her.

She realised that Chad was still looking down at her, his
expression faintly bemused. 'You were saving yourself
until you married him?' he asked with a faintly mocking
smile; but she sensed an earnestness underneath, a genuine
curiosity.

And because of that, she tried to answer honestly. 'I
didn't think of it that way,' she admitted, her brow
puckering in thought. 'I guess I just wasn't ready to—to
make that final commitment . . . Which is why I'm here
now and Jonathan is back in Sydney.'

'Ah, yes . . .' Chad nodded slowly. 'You and your
friend Jonathan didn't see eye to eye about your work, if I
recall . . .'

Her work. They were back to that.

'Chad——' This time she mustn't let him divert her.
There had to be an end to the secrets, the evasions, if
anything true and lasting was to grow between them.
'Chad, you must let me tell you about my work. About
what I—about what I really do for a living.'

'Ah, yes . . . you were saying something before about
not being quite honest with me.' His expression was
quizzical now, and faintly bemused. 'If you're about to tell
me you make your living as a nude model, I simply won't
believe you,' he said languidly.

She giggled. She couldn't help it. 'How could I possibly
do that?' she countered, feigning a pout. 'A girl with a
tattoo.'

'Ah, yes, of course . . . your tattoo.' He nodded
gravely. 'Well, if it's not that, let me see . . .' He stroked
his chin. 'What else could a beautiful girl like you be doing
that you haven't been game enough to own up to? I
shudder to think.'

He didn't look at all worried, she realised. Quite the
reverse. She had to gulp down a surge of emotion at the
thought. Did it mean that he trusted her, no matter what?
Did it mean that he knew her well enough by now to know
that what she was about to own up to wouldn't be
anything too shameful, too objectionable?

On the other hand . . . She drew in a deep breath. When he learned the truth, would he be hurt, angry, disillusioned at the thought that she had been blatantly deceiving him all this time?

Attack, she thought, rallying, is the best form of defence . . .

'It's not that I wasn't game enough to tell you,' she said spiritedly. 'I didn't tell you because I wanted to teach you a lesson.'

His brow rose. 'Let me guess,' he drawled. 'You wanted to teach me to have respect for models. Am I getting warm?'

'I wanted you to have respect for *me*—regardless of whether I was a model or not!' she corrected. 'You struck me as being so quick to judge people by the kind of work they happen to do . . . I wanted to make you see that—well, that you should get to know and like people for themselves, rather than lumping them all under the label "despised model", or whatever. They's why I—I didn't tell you . . . quite everything,' she admitted. Which is an understatement, she thought with a twist of her lips.

'So what have you been hiding from me?' he asked, eyeing her narrowly. 'If it's not the type of modelling you do . . . ah!' He clicked his fingers. 'I recall now . . . you implied once that you did something else as well, and for some reason I neglected to follow it up. Or did you divert me?' he accused gently. 'So what else is it that you do, Miss Hayes? Are you going to tell me now—or am I going to have to force it out of you?' He let his hand slide to her throat and she felt the pressure of his thumb-tip on her windpipe.

'It's not exactly something else,' she confessed, realising she was risking her neck by prevaricating further. 'It's the *only* thing I do. You see, I'm not really a model at all.'

There! It was out at last. Now, was he going to throttle her—or let her explain?

'I think you had better explain,' Chad said as if he'd read the exact words in her mind. His thumb-tip was no longer resting on her windpipe; it was now lingering just above her collarbone. Maybe he'd throttle her later—after she had explained.

'I had never met Zara Magatelli before the day of the fashion parade,' she admitted. 'She just happened to see me by the pool that day and begged me to fill in for one of her models who'd had to drop out. I agreed . . . reluctantly. Having never modelled before in my life. Nor ever had the faintest urge to.'

'Just what *do* you do for a living?' Chad asked slowly, his grey eyes darkening, smouldering under his heavy brows. He looked rather dangerous, she thought, and although she suspected it was just an act, she decided, in view of his hovering thumb-tip, that she'd better tell him now, quick-smart.

She swallowed. 'I'm a doctor, Chad.'

Her announcement was greeted with dead silence. Chad's face showed no reaction whatsoever. She gulped nervously. Perhaps it's the shock, she thought, wondering whether that was a good or a bad sign. Please don't turn away from me, Chad, she begged silently, as swift alarm gripped her. This should bring us closer together, not tear us apart. Please don't see it as deception, as dishonesty. See it for what it was. As a misguided—if you like—attempt to make you like me for myself.

But she could feel his withdrawal; she could feel it in the sudden stiffening of his body, in the way he let his hand slide away, as if he had no desire to touch her any more, lovingly, teasingly, or in any other way.

And then his voice lashed her, his anger, his resentment clearly evident, not only in his voice, but in the hard, reproachful glitter of his eyes. 'You've been stringing me along all this time, letting me think——*Why didn't you tell me sooner?*'

The coldness lacing his words brought a painful constriction to her throat, and a huskiness to her voice. 'Chad, things have been happening so fast——' she began, only to let her voice trail despondently away. Her reasons for hiding the truth from him seemed, at best, flimsy now, almost puerile in fact. But, puerile or not, surely Chad could understand her motives, if he knew and understood her at all? She had already explained that she had wanted to teach him a lesson. He must realise that she would have confided in him much earlier if he hadn't been so arrogant and unreasonable about models—and if he hadn't made exasperating, chauvinistic assumptions about *her*, in particular.

'Yes, far too fast,' agreed Chad bitingly, stifling the defence that rose to her lips. 'I think we've both been guilty on that score.' Was he regretting those heated kisses just now, the intimacies they had shared, the hinted admissions? Pain such as she had never known before knifed through her.

He shook his head, his face tightening. 'If you've deceived me about this, what else have you been less than honest about?' Before she could react, or utter a denial, he brought his face close to hers to demand angrily, 'Do you know what you really want, Gemma? I wonder.' His lips were only a breath away from hers, but she saw no softness there, nor in the smouldering eyes. His fingers were digging painfully into the flesh of her shoulders, but she didn't struggle, didn't cry out; she barely even noticed.

'Wh-what do you mean?' she whispered. Was he referring to him, to her career, or to Jonathan? Why had everything suddenly gone wrong? She had been so sure he would understand!

He shook her slightly, exasperation cracking the icy veneer. 'Well? Are you going to tell me more about this medical career you've been keeping so quiet about? Are you actually practising, or what?'

She bit her lip. 'I've just left the hospital where I was a resident for the past two years. A—a private clinic has offered me a partnership in Sydney, but—' She swallowed. 'I needed a break before committing myself . . .'

Before committing myself . . . Her mind echoed the words dully. She had been ready enough a moment ago to commit herself to loving Chad. Now she wondered, with a pang, if she had been carried away too fast, too soon, by her emotions. Perhaps she didn't know Chad as well as she had thought. She felt let down—saddened, disappointed—that he had reacted the way he had. Didn't he want her now that he knew she was a doctor? Now that he saw her as someone who was as committed to her work as he was to his?

His hands were still gripping her shoulders, his face still close to hers, still stormy. Suddenly he brought his head down and pressed his lips to hers, bruisingly, without tenderness. And then he released her abruptly, and stood up.

'I think we both have some hard thinking to do,' he said, and his eyes as he looked down at her were shadowed and remote.

'Chad——' His name was torn from her. In that second, she realised it made no difference how well or how little she knew him, or how soon, how quickly, she had lost her heart. She still loved him, and always would . . . nothing could change that. The thought of losing him now was unthinkable—unbearable. With a faint sob, she reached out to him, hiding a sigh when Chad made no move to accept the hand she offered him. But she saw a wavering in his eye, and something else that she would have sworn was a spark of the same passion that had blazed there quite openly earlier on, when she had brazenly offered him her body—and her love.

She looked up at him now, as she had then, invitingly, shamelessly, in the hope that they could forget the pain, the doubts, the deceptions of the past, in the bliss of each other's arms . . .

'Don't think it's not tempting,' Chad said, reading her mind as he so often could; but his expression as he stood over her was as grim and uncompromising as his tone.

She gulped down a wave of guilt, her cheeks flushed with shame. What must he think of her—a doctor, like himself—enticing him like this, urging him to break his Hippocratic oath? She was still his patient, first and foremost.

'Chad, I'm sorry.' She withdrew her hand. She must give him time to think things out for himself, without emotions, passions, getting in the way.

'I'll be in my studio for a while.' With that, Chad turned away from her rather abruptly, and strode to the door with a muttered, 'Sleep tight.'

Watching him go, she felt a wave of panic. 'Chad!' she called after him, her voice hoarse, barely audible. 'I never meant to hurt you . . .'

He paused in the doorway. 'No . . . I know that,' he said in a gentler tone. But his voice, his eyes, were still cool. 'See you in the morning,' were the last words she heard as he turned on his heel and marched out, pulling the door shut behind him.

CHAPTER TEN

IT MUST have been hours before she slept, drifting at long last into a dream-tossed, restless oblivion. She woke heavy-eyed and headachey, and conscious of an uneasy, churned-up feeling inside.

'Chad . . .' Her sleep-fogged brain was instantly crystal-clear—painfully so. She sat up, listening for a sound from the other room, wondering if Chad had slept on his camp stretcher outside her door, or if he had slept elsewhere. Or had he stayed up all night in his studio?

The twittering and shrilling of the birds outside made it difficult to hear anything else, but as far as she could tell there was dead silence in the next room.

She slipped out of bed and pulled on the clothes Melanie had brought for her. Then she tiptoed across the room and peeped out. There was no sign of Chad—nor, for that matter, of any camp stretcher.

She couldn't find him in the kitchen, either. There were no cups or dishes in the sink, which seemed to suggest he hadn't had his breakfast yet.

She poked her head out of the front door and saw the mini-moke parked under a tree. So he hadn't been summoned away on a call. And it was far too early for his morning surgery to have started.

'Chad,' she called tentatively. Then, a little louder, 'Chad, are you out there?'

He emerged almost at once from the creeper-covered iron shed opposite. He had a paintbrush in his hand—and, incredibly, a smile on his lips. A rather abashed one, but a smile none the less.

'Good morning. You're awake early.' His eyes seemed to light up when he saw her—unless it was just the misty morning sunlight catching him in the eye.

She heard herself asking, to cover a rush of nervousness, 'Chad, where did you sleep last night?

'I fell asleep on the sofa.' He rubbed his neck. 'I have a crick in my neck to prove it.'

'Oh, Chad . . .' She wanted to offer to rub it for him, but uncertainty, and an unaccustomed shyness, prevented her. He must have come back inside, sat down on the sofa to mull things over, and dropped off where he sat. *Your* fault, Gemma Hayes, she berated herself.

'Chad . . .' Her voice sobered. 'I'm sorry . . . it was stupid of me to let you go on thinking——' She stopped, spread her hands, and tried again. 'I never meant——'

'I know,' he broke in gently. 'You never meant to lie, cheat and deceive. Only to teach me a lesson.' A glitter of silver flared in his grey eyes. Could it possibly be amusement? 'Well, at least you've proved you're consistent,' he added drily.

'Consistent?' she echoed warily.

'Yes, you've been continually surprising me from the moment we met. Last night you did it again.'

She bit her lip, hope flaring. 'Then you—you're not mad at me any more?'

'No, I'm not mad at you. I'm afraid I . . . over-reacted last night.'

She swallowed her relief. 'Chad, it was wrong of me

not to tell you sooner. Can you forgive me?'

His lip curved a trifle. 'I'm making a supreme effort.'
She saw a glint in his eye, humour flickering in the grey.
'I think I'm beginning to understand the way your
funny little mind works,' he said. 'You were trying to
redress what you saw as an injustice on my part. You
wanted me to like you for yourself—regardless of what
you do for a living. That was it, wasn't it?'

She nodded, opening her lips to speak. But Chad held
up a finger.

'And by letting me go on thinking you were a model,
you were putting me to the severest test.' He quirked an
eyebrow at her. 'How would I have learned the error of
my ways if you had told me any earlier?'

'Now you're laughing at me.'

'On the contrary—if I'm laughing at anyone, it's at
myself. You completely fooled me, you little vixen. And
yet—there was always something . . .' A reflective light
came into his eyes. 'A number of things that didn't add
up before are now starting to make sense . . .'

She flushed, guessing he had spent much of the night
throwing his mind back, going over their every moment
together.

'I see now that it wasn't modelling your fiancé
objected to but . . . medicine.' Chad paused, tapping his
chin. 'I take it he didn't like you being a doctor?'

'Oh, he never minded me being a "doctor".' With a
half-smile, Gemma sketched quotataion marks in the air
with her fore-fingers. 'He was just against me accepting
the partnership I'd been offered. He wanted me to do
casual locum work—if I had to practise medicine at all.'

'And that's why you told him you wouldn't marry
him?' As he asked the question, Chad gazed at the

paintbrush in his hand as if he had just realised it was
there.

'We both wanted different things.' She shrugged
impatiently. 'Chad, don't let's talk about Jonathan. He's
not a part of my life any more . . .'

'That's good.' Raising his eyes, Chad reached out with
his free hand to brush her hair back from her face. 'I don't
believe in sharing my women.' He spoke lightly, almost
making a joke of it, but her heart leapt at his words. 'My
women . . .' And hadn't he asked, last night, 'Are you the
woman I've been looking for all my life?'

Suddenly she realised she was smiling. Hope, happiness,
love, relief, were mingled together in the smile.

Chad slid his hand down under her chin and tilted her
head back. 'You've been having the time of your life,
haven't you, pulling the wool over my eyes?'

Her smile wavered. 'Chad, it wasn't like that at all—
truly.' She looked up at him appealingly, and saw that his
eyes were bright with laughter. He's enjoying this, she
realised. Extracting penance from me. If he thinks I'm
going to get down on my knees and beg forgiveness——

'You'd like to see me beg, wouldn't you? Just as I did
before . . .' Her dark eyes flashed with a return of their old
fire. 'Well, Dr Rivers, let me tell you . . . I never beg before
breakfast.'

'A pity.' Chad removed his hand from her chin and
patted her cheek. He was grinning openly now. 'Give me
five minutes to clean up in here, and I'll come in and get
you some,' he said.

'No, no . . . kindly allow me, sir,' she said with a mock
bow, and ducked back into the house. She soon found
where everything was, and by the time Chad came in she
had the table set and the breakfast prepared.

'Mm . . . pancakes!' Chad looked impressed. 'And I thought you said you couldn't cook.'

'I found a packet of pancake mix in the cupboard,' she confessed. 'I just followed the instructions. I reckon all cooking must be the same . . . just following instructions. Nothing too difficult about that. Fruit salad to follow,' she said, screwing up her nose in an expression that was half proud, half smug.

Chad threw back his head and laughed. 'Gemma Hayes, you're incorrigible. I don't believe there's anything you wouldn't try your hand at. Is there?'

'Lots of things. Painting, for one. I know my limits. But I'd be happy to mix your paints or pose for you.'

'That's very kind of you. Mix my paints by all means . . . even pose for me if you wish. It would give me great delight to sit contemplating you all day . . .' Her heart soared at the tenderness in his voice, and in his eyes, a tenderness she had never expected to see or hear again. 'But don't expect me to paint you. As I've said before, I'm hopeless at human faces and figures. Anyway, I've finished painting for this morning,' he said. 'And I have another idea. Two ideas.'

'The first?' she asked encouragingly. That warm glow in his eyes was making her feel quite heady. But was it only passion, only lust, that he felt for her? Or was it something deeper? Could he . . . She caught her breath. Was it possible that he was beginning to love her the way she loved him—with his heart, mind, body and soul? She hardly dared think it possible.

'How about an intimate dinner for two by candlelight tonight?' Chad suggested, smiling down at her with that same melting look in his eyes—a look she couldn't believe was mere lust. Lust was a selfish emotion. What she saw in Chad's eyes was something far more tender, far more giving. 'At your place?' he asked.

'At my place,' she agreed hoarsely. Where I'll no longer be your patient, she thought, wondering dreamily if Chad was having the same thought. 'I'll even do the cooking,' she offered.

'That should be interesting.' For a second he brought his face close to hers, his lips an aching breath away—only to draw back abruptly, with a half-laugh, half-groan, reaching out instead, with infinite gentleness, to touch his hand to her cheek.

She let out a faint sigh. Wasn't he game to kiss her? There was a thickness in his voice that suggested he might not entirely trust himself. She was tempted to put him to the test, but medical ethics won out. While she was still here in Chad's house—on this particular occasion, at any rate—she must remember that she was his patient. Those were the ground rules. Once she was back in her bure, the situation would be altogether different . . .

'And your second idea?' she asked a trifle unsteadily.

He let his hand fall to her shoulder. 'There's a secluded little beach below my house . . . How about we take a stroll down there after breakfast? We could have a morning dip before I take you back to your bure and go on to the surgery.'

'I—I don't have my swimsuit with me,' she said, wondering why her pulse-rate had quickened. If the beach was as secluded as Chad said, he might not care if . . . he might even expect . . . She felt her colour rising at the images that leapt into her mind.

'I wouldn't look if you wanted to go in without one,' Chad offered blithely. 'Even if I did . . .' A wicked gleam shone for a moment in his eye. 'You must know, being a doctor yourself, that I wouldn't turn a hair at the sight of a beautiful naked female. Seeing a good-looking male in the same state wouldn't bother you either, would it?' he asked provocatively.

Her heartbeat was going haywire—she felt as if she had dozens of crazed moths inside her. 'If you were the male in question, it just might,' she admitted frankly. She looked up at him archly. 'Nice to know you yourself wouldn't turn a hair, though.'

Something glinted in Chad's eye. 'On second thoughts, maybe we'd better stick to walking, just for today. I'm not so sure I wouldn't turn a hair at that.' His eyes slid down her slender body, and she felt as if he were undressing her there and then. Only her love and her respect for Chad's professional integrity kept her from deliberately taunting him further—tempted as she was. This was a small community, she had to remember, and word must have got around by now—through Melanie, if not from Chad himself—that she was staying here at the doctor's cottage until she had fully recovered from her knock on the head.

'I think just a walk would be a good idea,' she agreed primly. That's the girl, Gemma . . . be good. Behave yourself. Think of Dr Rivers' reputation. Once you're out from under his professional mantle, though, and no longer his patient . . . well, no one could object to the doctor having a woman friend—could they? She shivered with joyous atnicipation.

So, instead of going for a swim, they just walked . . . and they talked . . . and they behaved—more or less. Chad did catch hold of her hand as they strolled along the crescent of bright yellow sand bordering the secluded bay and paddled in the crystal-clear shallows . . . and he did at one stage slip his arm around her waist, so that she was

suffocatingly conscious of his warm fingers kneading her
flesh through her thin cotton shirt . . . and on their way up
the hill from the beach he did press her to him just once in
the shade of a fruit-laden paw-paw tree, and kiss her
hungrily, if far too briefly, on the lips, setting her pulses
racing. But that was it. Models of decorum, Gemma
reflected whimsically. Ah, but just wait until tonight . . .
That candlelit dinner for two in my bure is going to be the
prelude to something big . . . I can feel it!

When Chad dropped her off at her bure on his way to
his surgery, he said, 'I'll pop in at lunch time and see how
you are.' He did more than that. In between his morning
and afternoon surgery, he took her for a pleasant sail
round the island, dropping anchor just once, in the same
secluded bay they had visited that morning, to have a
cooling dip in the sea—wearing stinger suits as a
precaution. Gemma couldn't help wondering, with a
delicious ripple down her spine, if they were protecting
themselves from the dangers of the deep . . , or from each
other.

During those pleasant hours, they chatted about their
work, and about medicine in general, and it felt
marvellous being able to talk openly about it at last. When
Chad dropped her back at the marina before rushing off
to his afternoon surgery, Gemma, instead of heading for
the beach or the pool, did some food shopping and then
hastened back to her bure to prepare dinner for the
evening. She wanted it to be really special . . . an evening
to remember. She planned to have a simple, delicious meal
of fresh prawns, ripe avocados, leafy green vegetables, and
firm rosy tomatoes, with fresh fruit and cream for dessert.
She had bought a couple of bottles of Chardonnay, which
she now had chilling in the fridge, and had selected a

bright red candle for the centre of the table. On either side, in two small glasses, she placed sprigs of red bouganvillaea.

She spent the rest of the afternoon pampering herself—washing her hair under the shower and blow-waving it into soft silvery-blonde waves, painting her fingernails and toenails, experimenting with different eyeshadows and settling on an earthy colour which enhanced the brown of her eyes, and trying on several dresses before deciding on a yellow across-the-shoulder sundress, which left one tanned shoulder delectably bare.

Just as she was inspecting the final result in her bedroom mirror, there was a knock on the outside door.

'Come in, Chad. You're early,' she called, tripping across the carpet to meet him at the door.

'Come in, *Chad*?'

The voice was familiar, but it wasn't Chad's voice.

Her smile froze on her lips. No . . . it couldn't be! Not here . . . not *now*.

'Jonathan . . . what are you doing here?' Dazedly, she waved him inside.

He was looking her up and down, his eyes cool, almost hostile. Knowing him the way she did, she knew the coolness was to hide his hurt, his disappointment. He didn't have to look very far or very closely to see that she was expecting company . . . *male* company. And she had called him Chad.

'Jonathan, I haven't changed my mind,' she blurted out, deciding to take the initiative. 'And nothing you say will——'

'I didn't expect you would,' Jonathan cut in, shrugging resignedly. 'That's why I came, Gemmy . . .' His voice trailed off as a sharp rap sounded at the front door. His

pale grey-blue eyes—no wonder I couldn't remember them
clearly, Gemma thought irrelevantly: there's really nothing
remarkable about them at all—looked faintly chagrined as
he turned his head. As she swept past him to the door, she
saw his handsome face tighten.

Oh, Jonathan, she thought, sighing. If only you had
given me some warning! I was so looking forward to this
evening alone with Chad.

Chad's smile was nearly her undoing. She smiled
back—weakly.

'Chad, come in,' she invited, wishing she didn't feel so
nervous. Darn it, there was no need. Now that Jonathan
knew that she hadn't changed her mind about anything, he
would want to leave—surely? There would be no point in
him lingering—especially now that Chad had turned up.
She would introduce them, the three of them would
exchange a few pleasantries, and Jonathan would bow
out. First, of course, she would have to do the right thing
and invite him to join them for dinner . . . but he wouldn't
accept. A *ménage à trois* wouldn't suit Jonathan. It would
be pretty uncomfortable, for that matter, for all three of
them. If Jonathan wanted to speak to her alone before he
left the island, she would agree to see him in the morning.
But tonight she had promised to Chad . . . and she wasn't
going to let Jonathan spoil the evening she had planned.

But things didn't go quite as she had hoped. The
moment the introductions were over, Jonathan turned his
back on Chad and addressed Gemma as if the other man
didn't exist.

'As I was saying, Gemma,' he said through tight lips,
blithely going on from where he had left off when Chad
arrived, 'I didn't think—or expect—that you *would* have
changed your mind. That's why I came to you—to tell you

that I've changed mine. I can't——' he hesitated, eyeing Chad belligerently, 'I can't bear it without you, Gemma. You—you can take the Sydney partnership if you still want it. I'd rather have you working full-time than not have you at all.'

It was so unexpected that she could do nothing but just stare at him for a moment. He had been so adamant all along. She had never expected for one moment that he would be the one to back down.

'Jonathan, I——'

Her words were cut off abruptly. 'I can see you two have things to talk about . . . alone.' Chad's tone cut the air like ice. 'Goodbye, Gemma.' It was a cold, very final-sounding 'goodbye'. Gemma was aware of a choking panic rising in her throat. It was almost as if he were turning away from her without a fight . . . without any pain, any regrets at all.

'Chad——' she croaked as he turned on his heel. 'Chad!' she called after him in desperation, as the door slammed behind him.

As she started after him, Jonathan caught her arm. It was the roar of the mini-moke rather than Jonathan's restraining hand that brought her to a halt, her shoulders slumping. Jonathan swung her round and looked into her stricken face. His jaw tensed visibly, and he said, grating the words through his teeth, 'You didn't waste any time finding someone else. How far has it gone?'

Her frayed nerves made her react sharply, snapping at him, 'I haven't slept with him, if that's what you're asking.'

He chuckled nastily. 'You've never slept with me either, remember, and yet you told me you loved me and wanted to marry me.'

'I thought I did love you. And at one time I *did* want to marry you.'

'Did?' He leapt on the word. 'And what about now? Will you marry me, Gemma, now that you know I'm not asking you to give anything up? You couldn't have fallen out of love with me as quickly as this . . . *have* you?' he demanded, a muscle quivering at his jaw.

'Jonathan, I——' She swallowed, knowing what it must have cost Jonathan to change his mind and give in, when she knew that deep down he must still hate the idea of her taking that partnership. He must care for her more than she'd thought . . .

She sighed. Sadly, his sacrifice, his generosity, had come too late. It no longer mattered . . . because he, Jonathan, no longer mattered to her. It wasn't going to be easy to tell him, but tell him she must.

'Jonathan, please sit down,' she pleaded, but he shook his head impatiently.

'You haven't answered my question. You do still love me, don't you?' There was a thread of uneasiness in his tone. 'You will come back to me, won't you, Gemma? I've agreed to your accepting the partnership . . . that's what you want, isn't it?'

She took a deep breath. 'Jonathan, I'm touched—honestly. But——' She bit her lip. 'It's not as simple as that. It's not just the partnership—it never was. I didn't love you enough . . . I couldn't have—don't you see? If I had, I would have been prepared to compromise. I'd have worked something out—*anything*. But I wasn't. I've realised since I've been here that my feelings just weren't strong enough . . .' Involuntarily, her gaze flickered towards the door, a pensive look darkening her eyes.

Jonathan's eyes searched her face. 'Oh lord,' he

whispered, 'you love him, don't you? You've fallen for him—in just these few short days!' His fingers slackened on her arm. 'Does he love you?'

Gemma shook her head helplessly. 'I don't know,' she said honestly, her pained eyes meeting his. 'I thought he was beginning to, but . . .' She gulped, picturing Chad's face as he had turned away from her and walked out. His feelings couldn't have run very deep, for him to have walked away so easily. 'Anyway,' she said thinly, 'it doesn't make any difference, Jonathan . . . I did the right thing when I broke off our engagement. It would never have worked. Your instincts were right when you gave me that ultimatum. What you were really doing was testing me . . . to see just how strong my feelings were. And they weren't strong enough. Go back home, Jonathan, and find a girl who will make you happy. I'm not that girl.'

Jonathan didn't argue with her—he just looked thoughtful, and the faintest bit peeved. He had come up here expecting her, no doubt, to fall into his arms with gratitude and love, and he had to adjust to the fact that she hadn't. If he was hurt, his ego wouldn't allow him to show it. Or not much. Jonathan had a healthy ego—and he was an eminently practical man. It was probably already beginning to dawn on him that what she was saying was true. She was not the wife for him.

'I'm not going to beg, Gemma,' he said, and she hid a secret, rueful smile. Jonathan was offering her a last chance—but it was a half-hearted offer. He already knew, deep down, that it was over—and even if he didn't fully realise it yet, he accepted it. Jonathan didn't really want a career-wife; let alone a wife who loved him less than he loved her. And rightly so, Gemma thought, relieved that he was taking it as well as he was.

'I'm sorry you came all this way for nothing,' she said gently.

Jonathan nodded curtly. 'What do you intend to do?' he asked abruptly. 'Is your new love going to follow you down to Sydney? I take it you still intend to accept the partnership?'

'I don't know.' A spasm of doubt crossed her face. 'It all depends . . .' She hesitated, not wanting to hurt Jonathan further.

'On your new love, you mean?' he asked, making no attempt now to hide the bitterness in his voice.

With difficulty, she met his eyes. 'Jonathan, I've told you—I don't know what's going to happen yet. It—it's too early to say.' For all she knew, Chad could have turned his back on her for good. Perhaps he had intended to all along. Didn't they say that love was blind? Couldn't her love for Chad have made her read more into his attentions than were there?

No! She refused to believe that she meant nothing at all to Chad. Far better—far easier—to believe that he had bowed out because of what he had overheard . . . because he had witnessed Jonathan backing down and offering her marriage *and* a full-time career. By retiring gracefully, Chad was giving her a chance to accept.

But surely Chad knew her well enough by now to know that she would spurn her ex-fiancé's offer and send Jonathan packing? He must know she didn't love him . . . that it was he, Chad, whom she loved.

She frowned, biting her lip thoughtfully. Or had Chad turned away from her for deeper, more personal reasons: because he couldn't see a future with her, even with Jonathan out of the picture? After the failure of his marriage to Roxanne, Chad would be wary of tying himself to another full-time career-woman. He wouldn't want to risk a second failed marriage. How was he to know that she would be prepared to give up anything to be with him, that she would gladly turn down the Sydney partnership, that she would work as little or as much as he wanted her to—even give up practising altogether if he asked her to, so that they could be together, and so that, when the time came, she could devote herself to their children? How could he know? She had never had a chance to tell him!

Still, the thought gave her some hope. Surely, once she let Chad know that she had refused Jonathan's offer, and that she was prepared to turn her back on the Sydney practice to stay up here with him, if he wanted her to, Chad would gather her in his arms and never let her go? Assuming he loved her and wanted her, of course. And he must! He *must*! She wouldn't be too proud to declare herself first—to tell him she loved him . . . wanted him . . . needed him. She would do anything. But she couldn't lose him—she just couldn't!

'You've forgotten I'm here already, haven't you?' Jonathan accused, his voice, half resigned, half resentful, breaking into her thoughts. 'If you could see the look in your eyes . . . You never looked like that with me,' he complained. His gaze flicked to the table, romantically set for two. 'I can see I arrived at the wrong moment—I should never have come.'

'Jonathan, it was very generous of you to—to make the offer you did.' She reached out impulsively and touched his arm, dropping it as she felt him flinch. She hadn't meant the gesture to appear patronising. 'You've been a wonderful friend,' she added sincerely, 'and I'm fond of you. I always will be. But believe me, I've done the right thing for both of us. You'll see. Now go home and get on with your life . . . and I wish you the best of luck.'

'Thanks.' He blew out a sigh. Perhaps it was partly relief, now that the doubts, the hopes, the conflicts were over. 'Well, I guess you're right . . . not much point dragging this out. I'll bow out gracefully and you can go and find your . . . friend. Any message for your parents? They said they'd only had one card from you.'

'I know, and tell them I'm sorry . . . I guess I've had other things on my mind these past few days. I'll call them in a day or so . . . I promise. Meanwhile, tell them I'm fine.'

'I can see that.' A pensive, grudging admiration crept into his eyes. 'I've never seen you looking lovelier. There's a new quality about you . . . I don't know.' He shrugged. 'Love does things for you, Gemma.' His tone was rueful, and the irony of his words didn't escape her. 'Well, goodbye . . . and I wish *you* luck.'

She looked at him gratefully. 'Goodbye, Jonathan— and thank you . . . I might need it,' she admitted with a poignant smile.

Next moment she was standing alone, the silence swirling around her like thick smoke. Her sense of humour brought a reluctant smile to her lips. It wasn't every day that the only two men in your life walked out on you within minutes of each other!

You're not getting away that easily, Chad Rivers, she thought, springing into action. She found his home number and dialled feverishly. Hearing the dialling tone, she chewed anxiously on her lip, eager to hear his familiar voice—wary perhaps, at first, but glad, relieved, surely, to hear from her? She hung on and on and on. There was no answer. Thinking that in her haste she could have dialled wrongly, she tried again, with the same result. Not

expecting Chad to be at his surgery at this hour, but
thinking it was worth a try anyway, she dialled his surgery
number, but he wasn't there either.

Recalling his stony face as he had marched out, she
thought of the bars along the marina. A possibility. She
decided to take a stroll to the harbour in the hope of
catching sight of his red mini-moke.

The sun was setting in a blaze of flaming orange as she
jogged along the road to the marina. Another glorious
night. If she could only find Chad, there was still time for
him to dine at her bure . . . still time for her romantic
dinner by candlelight. The food was ready and waiting,
chilling nicely in the refrigerator alongside the bottles of
Chardonnay.

She spent the next half-hour scouring the harbour-front.
There was no sign of Chad's mini-moke outside any of the
bars or cafés or restaurants, but she peeped inside each one
anyway, even weaving her way through a few of the more
crowded ones to make a thorough search, braving the
frowns when she walked out again without even buying a
drink.

Wouldn't her old mates back home be chortling, she
reflected idly, if they could see this side of Gemma Hayes?
Prowling around bars looking for a man! How the mighty
are fallen!

As for herself, she was feeling less amused by the
minute. 'Chad, where are you?' she muttered aloud,
having exhausted her last hope. At one of the resort
restaurants, perhaps? Unlikely. Chad tended to steer clear
of the resort unless he was specifically meeting someone,
or was obliged to attend an official function.

Could he have gone to the Danes? Her eyes flickered to
the staff block on the rise overlooking the harbour.

Desperation stifled her pride. She had to find Chad and tell him about Jonathan. Now . . . tonight!

By now dusk had fallen, but there were plenty of lights to guide her way. In the car park below the block of units, she pulled up sharply. A red mini-moke was parked near the front entrance. Chad's?

Swallowing hard, she forced her legs to keep on walking. A woman she had met once at the resort— someone in public relations, she dimly recalled—almost collided with her as she stepped inside the front entrance.

'I—I'm looking for the Danes,' Gemma said hastily, to explain why she was there.

'They're not home,' the woman said promptly. 'Nick's away—he had to fly down to Sydney for a couple of days on business. And I just saw Melanie leaving a while ago. Heading for the marina with Dr Rivers.'

The marina? With *Chad*?

'I know it was the doc,' the woman added as Gemma chewed on her lip, 'because he had his arm around her and I looked twice just to see who it was.' She gave a chuckle. 'Don't get me wrong . . . it didn't mean anything. The doc's a good friend of theirs. And Melanie's his nurse, you know.'

'Yes, I know.' She heard the hollowness in her voice and hoped the woman wouldn't notice. Chad had gone straight to Melanie! And Nick was away for the night . . .

Gemma, don't jump to conclusions . . . She grasped at reason. They could have had an urgent call; Chad could have needed the help of his nurse.

She thanked the woman thinly, and turned away. She hardly knew where she was walking, until she ended up back at the marina. Turning her back on the bars and cafés, she ran her eyes restlessly over the boats silhouetted

against the evening sky. And realised that Chad's yacht
was missing! Her heart lurched in a sick nosedive. Chad
and Melanie must have gone off together in the yacht . . .
But where? *Why*?

Pointless to speculate. There could be a dozen reasons.
Only one was worth worrying about . . . and that was the
one reason she refused to dwell on. She'd only make her
life a misery if she did.

With a sigh, she turned on her heel and headed back to
her lonely bure.

CHAPTER ELEVEN

SHE picked at her breakfast without enthusiasm. She had hardly slept a wink overnight; her mind had kept on going over and over the possible reasons for Chad's sailing off with Melanie at that hour of the night. Logical, acceptable reasons vied with soul-destroying ones, the soul-destroying ones winning out. She might as well face it. Chad had walked out on her believing she would go back to Jonathan, and he had gone straight to Melanie for comfort . . .

How *could* he? She had thought he was genuinely beginning to care for her. Oh, Chad, no, you couldn't! Her heart screamed the denial. There had to be an explanation. Worried as she was, she couldn't believe that he would be so fickle, that he would turn so quickly from one woman to another. And yet, if he believed that she had left him . . .

She would just have to find him as quickly as possible and let him know that she had sent Jonathan away—for good.

Her feverish thoughts had raced on, all through the long, tortured night, as she planned what she would say to him, imagined what he would say to *her*, speculated on what would happen after that . . .

And now morning had arrived at last, and not only was she feeling worn out, her eyes heavy and deeply shadowed, her hair lank from her tossing and turning, but she still felt as tense, as tormented as ever, racked with restless impatience, and trembling with nervous anticipation. In desperation she pushed her breakfast aside and dialled Chad's home number.

She was disappointed, but not surprised when there was no answer. He—she refused to accept that it might be 'they'—would almost certainly have slept on the yacht last night, having sailed out so late. Perhaps, if she wandered down to the marina, she could keep an eye out for him sailing back. He would have to be back by ten, for his morning surgery.

But what if Melanie was on board? How could she bear to face Chad if he had already taken up with Melanie again? It would be too awful . . . too embarrassing for all three of them. No . . . she couldn't risk that. When she saw Chad, she must know that he was alone.

Not much point, in that case, hanging around his surgery either . . . Melanie would only be there as well. She sighed, and bit her lip. She guessed she could always wait around outside somewhere, out of sight, hoping to catch Chad alone when he left around midday; but she wasn't really the type who skulked in the shrubbery, spying on people! Better to visit his home after lunch and just hope that he would be there.

She decided not to phone him first this time. Chad might demand to know *why* she was calling him, and she didn't want to tell him about Jonathan over the phone. She wanted to be able to watch the changes in his expression when she told him she had sent Jonathan away, and that she was going to turn down the Sydney partnership offer. In the brightness of day, her qualms about Melanie were beginning to subside bit by bit. She was probably—hopefully—doing Chad a grave injustice.

How could he have looked into her eyes with so much
tenderness yesterday, how could he have uttered the words
he did, and then spent the night with another woman? No
matter how hurt he was, no matter how certain he might
have been that she was going to leave him, she couldn't
believe that of him. Surely he would wait first to hear what
she had decided to do?

She passed the waiting hours windsurfing on the bay,
followed by a long swim in the resort pool, striking
through the water from one end to the other until she was
worn out. But the physical activity was proving beneficial;
she felt more optimistic, more buoyant by the second.
Hadn't Chad asked her, 'Are you the woman I've been
looking for all my life?' Yes, she must think positively.
Chad had only left her with Jonathan last night because he
had been thinking of *her*; he hadn't wanted to put any
pressure on her. Today he would be waiting to hear,
hoping to hear, that she had sent Jonathan packing.

At midday she went back to her bure to change,
deliberately avoiding Chad's surgery on the way. In fact,
she took the long route, via the marina. She wanted to
check that Chad's boat was back. Not much point visiting
him at home if it wasn't.

That yacht's sleek lines leapt into her vision as if it were
the only boat in the harbour. The sight acted like a balm to
her taut nerves. Chad was back . . . just as she had known
and expected that he would be. Chad would never miss out
on his morning surgery—he was far too conscientious a
doctor.

With a lighter step, she hastened back to her bure,
grabbing a hunk of fresh pineapple from the kitchen and
devouring it before heading for the bathroom. She knew
she had plenty of time . . . afternoon surgery didn't start

until four. The only doubt she had was that Chad might
not have gone home after surgery. He could have decided
to have lunch along the harbour somewhere—although
surely she would have seen him or his red mini-moke if he
had—and afterwards he could be planning to go
swimming or sailing.

She recalled the secluded bay near his home. Surely, if
he intended to go swimming, he would go swimming there,
not in the resort pool or in the shallow bay off the resort?
As for going out sailing, well, she hadn't seen him on or
near his boat while she had been wandering along the
marina earlier. No . . . his home seemed the best bet.
Besides, if he was waiting to hear from her, he would
know that she would try to contact him at home.

She pushed from her mind the possibility that he could
be out on a call, or at a meeting, or visiting friends. All
that was in her mind right now was the thought of finding
him quickly and seeing his face light up when she told him
that Jonathan had gone.

It took her a few minutes to decide what to wear.
Eventually, she settled on a backless cotton sundress in a
cool green colour which set off her tan beautifully. She
gave her silvery-blonde hair a good brushing and left it
hanging loose, despite the afternoon's heat. Then, pulling
on a pair of flat white sandals, she grabbed her key, locked
up and sprinted up the road towards the bush track which
led to Chad's cottage.

Was it only days since she had battled her way along this
same path in the howling wind and the driving rain? It
seemed like weeks! Aeons! She had been seeking Chad on
that occasion too, with fear in her heart; fear of what she
might find . . . And now she was seeking him again, and
she felt no less fearful—even thought it was a different

kind of fear.

As she hurried along, a bicycle wobbled into sight around a bend in the track ahead, and in a lightning reaction Gemma leapt back into the shelter of a clump of gum trees before the rider could spy her.

Melanie!

The fears she had successfully managed to stifle came tumbling back—tenfold. Why would Melanie be visiting Chad *here,* at his secluded home in the bush, unless——

No! She tried to ignore the demon voice that was whispering evil thoughts in her ear. There had to be a logical explanation! She couldn't bear it otherwise . . .

Who are you kidding, you poor fool? the hateful voice persisted. Melanie's husband is away, remember? And last night she was seen with Chad's arm around her, before they sailed off into the night. Gemma's eyes darkened with pain. Oh, Chad, and I was beginning to give you the benefit of the doubt. What am I to believe now?

In her misery, she stayed hidden until Melanie was safely past and out of sight. What was she to do now? Keep going, pretending nothing had happened? Find Chad and hope that when he saw her and learned that Jonathan was out of her life, he would toss Melanie aside once and for all, and fall gladly back into her loving arms?

She stood indecisively, torn between pride, hurt, love, and a desperation she had never known before. She was prepared to stifle her pride, and even her hurt, but her love and her desperation she couldn't deny. They were what finally turned her firmly in the direction of Chad's house. She knew she had to go to him and settle her doubts once and for all. Loving him the way she did, she still clung to the hope that he would have an acceptable explanation, and she owed him the chance to offer it to her. She

wasn't going to lose him over a misunderstanding, if that
was all it was. She had read enough romantic novels to
know the trouble misunderstandings could lead to.

A blanket of low cloud hung overhead, hiding the sun.
The hot, humid air was heavy with tropical scents. She
breathed in deeply as she hurried along, relishing the
warm, moist, sweet, spicy, tropical tang. How quickly she
had come to feel at home up here in the tropics, despite the
steamy autumn heat. Or did she only feel at home because
Chad was here? She sighed, knowing in her heart that it
was true. I would follow you anywhere, Chad Rivers . . .
Through fire or snow or the densest jungle. Even through
a cave full of spiders—though I might be a jibbering wreck
at the end of it!

When she spied Chad's cottage up ahead, she ran her
tongue nervously over her lips. Would he *want* her to
follow him anywhere—even through a cave full of
spiders? She straightened her shoulders and thrust out her
chin. Enough of this defeatist talk! She wasn't going to
lose her courage now—or her optimisim.

The cockatoos were making their usual din as she
approached the house. Would she too feel like screeching
in the coming minutes? With frustration if Chad wasn't
there . . . with joyous delight if he was. Or . . . with fury
and despair if Chad made it clear that he didn't want her—
that he never had wanted her, that he'd just been having a
bit of harmless fun with her all the time—the way he liked
having fun with Melanie while her husband was out of the
way . . .

Chad's ivy-clad 'studio' caught her eye, and she realised
that it was because the old timber door was hanging open.
Had Chad decided to do some painting rather than go
down to the beach for a swim—or whatever else he might

in her fevered imagination have been doing with Melanie?

She felt her spirits lift. Perhaps Melanie had simply dropped in to look at the seascape he'd been painting . . . If that were the case, thank goodness she hadn't panicked and turned back!

She tiptoed to the door and peeped in. And felt a swift stab of disappointment when she saw that the studio was empty. But Chad *had* been painting . . . There was a canvas on the easel, and she could smell fresh paint.

Just as she was about to back out again and go looking for him in the house, her gaze leapt back to the canvas. It was not the seascape he had been working on the other day. It was a full-length portrait of a young woman.

A *portrait*! But Chad had sworn that he never painted portraits, that he was hopeless at them!

Heart hammering, she moved closer, recoiling as she bent over the canvas. The girl in the portrait was Melanie Dane! She was barefoot and smiling, and she looked unusually seductive in a boldly patterned sarong slit to the thigh. Gemma felt a painful tightening in her throat. For someone who had declared more than once that he never painted portraits, Chad had achieved a remarkable likeness. Almost a *loving* likeness, she reflected with poignant bitterness. The tropical island background, while it was lush and realistic, had a mistiness about it, as if Chad had deliberately intended that the background should not overshadow the main subject.

He must have been secretly working on this portrait for days! For weeks, for all she knew. Resentment rumbled through her. Why had Chad lied to her? Why had to told her he never painted portraits, that he was hopeless at painting anything but seascapes and landscapes?

Because he didn't want anyone to know he was painting

another man's wife? Because he didn't want anyone to guess that he was having an *affair* with another man's wife?

She felt sick in the heart as she turned away. No use fooling herself any longer. She should have taken notice of the warning signals from the beginning. Chad wasn't looking for a long-term relationship, let alone marriage. He had made a mistake once, and he didn't intend to repeat it. To him, she had been no more than an amusing distraction. The moment Chad knew that her man had come back to claim her, he had bowed out without a second thought and had blithely taken up again with his safely married nurse-receptionist!

Tears blurred Gemma's eyes as she stumbled away, giving Chad's cottage a wide berth as she headed back to the track. Whoever said that love was blind had sure known what he or she was talking about!

Goodbye, Chad, she muttered under her breath, and started running, wanting only to put distance between them now. As soon as she reached her bure she would make arrangements to leave the island. Both Chad and Jonathan were out of her life now. Men, period, were out of her life. She might as well go back to Sydney and accept the offered partnership. As for Chad, she had no compunction about leaving without saying goodbye face to face. *He* wouldn't care, and it would only be unbearably painful for her. Once she was safely home, she would write a letter thanking him politely for his kindness during her stay. In a letter, she would be able to pick her words with care, never letting him know what he had done to her.

Over the sound of her pounding footsteps, she heard others, like a ghostly echo of her own. Then she heard someone calling her name. At first she thought it was her imagination . . . that in her despair she was dreaming up Chad's voice, calling her back. Then, with a jolt, she realised it really *was* Chad's voice, and her heart sank to her toes. She had no wish to face Chad now!

Pausing, she turned slowly, reluctantly, her true expression hidden behind a self-protective, bravely smiling mask.

'Oh, so you were home after all,' she said in a coolly offhand tone that was a triumph of deception.

'Yes . . . funny, I didn't hear you at the door.' His expression was as guarded as her own. They were like polite strangers! He looked a little tired, she thought, and her lips tightened. It must have been a torrid night out there on the water with Melanie Dane!

Chad was still speaking, she realised, his tone detached, his eyes cool. 'I was heading back to the studio when I saw you sprinting away. Came to say goodbye, did you?'

Her heart twisted. It was obvious Chad had no intention of asking her to stay. And why should he? He didn't love her; he had shown that by running back to Melanie. Not only had he taken up with Melanie again, he was also secretly painting her portrait! That was the part that hurt most of all . . . the fact that Chad had lied to her, that he had deceived her. 'I never paint portraits,' he had stated flatly. 'I would paint you if I could . . .' And all the while he had been planning to paint, or had already started to paint, Melanie instead!

'That's right,' she managed to answer coolly, trying not to think what the sight of him was doing to her. Despite her inner misery, she felt an almost overwhelming rush of love as she peered up into his face, examining for perhaps the last time the sensuous shape of his lips, the strong curve of his jaw, the faint lines radiating from the silvery-grey eyes that had so recently looked into hers with tenderness—a tenderness that her own wishful thinking had mistaken for something deeper. She swallowed hard before she spoke again. Even then, there was a faint waver in her voice. 'And I—I wanted to thank you, Chad. You—you've been very g-good to me.' Damn it, why was she stuttering? Think about Melanie, you weak fool . . . that will soon cure your stutters.

'I was surprised to see you still here.' His own eyes seemed to be examining her face as carefully as she was examining his. 'I thought you would have left by now . . . with your fiancé.'

I'll bet you're surprised to see me, Dr Rivers, she agreed silently, her eyes smudged with bitterness. I nearly caught you with your other woman . . . Aloud she said, tossing her head, 'I passed Melanie on the way here.' Let him know that she knew what was going on! 'I saw the portrait, too,' she told him. 'It's very good. Incredibly good—for someone who never paints portraits.'

'Oh, I didn't paint that portrait,' Chad said calmly.

Her eyes sharpened. 'Next you'll be saying Melanie painted it herself,' she mocked. 'It had to be one of you . . . I *saw* it, Chad. The paint's still wet.'

'The *background's* still wet,' Chad corrected. He was looking at her oddly, as if puzzled by her tone. 'That's what I've been working on . . . just the tropical island background. Another artist painted the actual portrait . . . sadly leaving the background unfinished.'

Gemma swallowed—hard. Being the intelligent woman she was, she realised in an instant that she had made a clanging mistake. About one thing at least. Chad hadn't been lying when he'd told her he never painted portraits.

Just as he wasn't lying now when he said that someone else had painted that portrait of Melanie . . . And it wasn't too hard to guess who had.

'You mean . . . your wife Roxanne painted the portrait of Melanie.' It was barely a question.

'That's right.' Chad's expression was unreadable as he glanced down at her. 'Roxanne met Melanie while she was staying here on the island, and offered to paint Melanie's portrait. Only she . . . never finished it.'

Gemma looked at him mutely. She felt like kicking herself. Why hadn't she guessed that the truth about the portrait must have been something like that? Because she'd been blinded by jealousy, that was why! And it was still there, niggling away at her. She waited for him to go on.

He obliged, standing tall and straight in front of her, the stiffness of his stance showing he was still as wary, as tense as she. 'Later, when Melanie came to work for me, I realised at once that she was the girl in the portrait Roxanne had left behind. When I offered Melanie the unfinished portrait, she asked me if I would finish it myself. Apparently Roxanne had mentioned to her that I dabbled in landscapes. Since painting was the last thing I felt like doing at the time, I suggested she find another artist. But Melanie insisted I keep the portrait until I felt up to finishing it myself. No doubt she thought it would be good therapy.' His lip quirked slightly. 'She might have changed her mind,' he added drily, 'if she'd known it was going to be two years before I took up painting again.'

Gemma recalled how delighted Melanie had been the other day when she'd heard that Chad was painting again. That must have been when she had asked Chad to work on the portrait. Or at least, on the unfinished background.

She saw Chad glance up at the sky, which by now was ominiously dark. 'We'd better head back to the house,' he said. His manner was still distant, his real thoughts carefully masked. 'We could be in for a drenching if we don't.' He steered her back along the track with his hand resting lightly on her waist, the tips of his fingers brushing the bare flesh at the base of her backless dress. His touch, light as it was, started her nerve-ends jumping and sent quivery impulses darting through her body, making her acutely, painfully aware of his nearness. It was both agony and ecstasy.

'She must be pleased you're working on her portrait at last.' With difficulty she found her voice, bringing the subject determinedly back to Melanie.

'After two years of being patient, she's now cracking the whip,' Chad agreed with a nod. 'She wants to give the portrait to Nick as a gift. As a surprise. Having just had it confirmed that she's pregnant.'

Gemma's eyes flew to his face. 'Oh, Chad, that's wonderful!' She felt elated and ashamed at the same time. Elated for Melanie; ashamed of her own foolish and, she realised now, unfounded suspicions. It was glaringly obvious now that Chad hadn't been playing around with Melanie at all. He had simply been working on her portrait. A portrait of the happy mother-to-be!

She chewed on her lip, letting her mind flit back. Melanie's jumpiness the other day must have been due to her uncertainty about whether or not she was pregnant. And when Melanie had turned sharply away from her as if she couldn't stand the sight of her in Chad's bed, the reason was more likely to have been that she couldn't stand the sight of anyone eating!

A fine doctor you turned out to be, Gemma Hayes . . .

Not recognising the symptoms of morning sickness! You were listening to your foolish, twisted little heart and no your head.

She heard a low roll of thunder and glanced round noting that they were barely a hop and a skip from the shelter of Chad's cottage.

What a fool she had been! As if Melanie would be playing round with the island doctor at a time like this—a the happiest time of her life!

'Yes, they've waited a long time.' The deep rumble of Chad's voice broke into her thoughts. 'Melanie tells me Nick plans to resign from his resort job when he gets back from Sydney. They're buying a charter-boat business—it's a dream they've had for some time.'

'I'm so pleased.' Perhaps next time, Gemma Hayes, you'll heed your own advice and not go jumping to conclusions! Somehow she knew now, without even needing to ask, that Chad had never at any time been involved with Melanie—except as a friend, and as a colleague, of course. And presumably as Melanie's family doctor.

'I looked for you last night,' she admitted rather sheepishly. 'After Jonathan left . . .'

She saw something flare in Chad's eyes. 'He's left?'

'You sound surprised. You didn't honestly think he'd stay once he knew I had no intention of taking him back, did you?' she asked, eyeing him archly.

'You don't intend getting back together? Even now that your fiancé has withdrawn what I understood was the major obstacle?' Chad's face was still closed, still wary.

'I wish you'd stop calling him my fiancé. He stopped being that a long time ago. And no, Jonathan's change of heart didn't change my mind in the slightest. I don't love him.' She looked up unblinkingly into Chad's face, letting her love for him shine from her eyes. This wasn't a moment for coyness. She loved Chad, she wanted him, she needed him . . . why bother to hide it any longer? If you want something badly enough, her parents had always impressed on her, go after it.

Chad's eyes were riveted to hers, and the play of emotions on his face made her heart turn over.

'Chad,' she breathed, drinking in his gaze as a desperate hope, a desperate longing swept through her.

It was at that precise moment that the rain came down—a deafeningly sharp tropical downpour that at any other time would have had them scuttling for shelter. But neither of them moved. Like two figures carved from stone, they simply stood there, facing one another in the thudding rain, letting the water stream down their faces and soak into their clothes, their eyes locked together, hers unashamedly, openly revealing her love, his bit by bit losing their wariness, and brimming with the tenderness she had glimpsed once or twice before Jonathan's arrival and had despaired of ever seeing again.

And then she was in his arms, her wet lips parting, ready for his kiss, her drenched body straining against his, tiny moans escaping her as she felt Chad's hand on her lower back, pressing her even closer. She squeezed her eyes shut against the stinging rain, and abandoned herself to the whirls of sensataion spiralling through her.

When Chad bent over and in a swift movement gathered her in his arms she gave a tiny gasp, of ecstasy rather than shock. She didn't resist as he carried her to his cottage. She clung to his neck as if she would never let him go, thinking lazily, I'm not your patient any more, Dr Rivers . . . There's nothing to stop us this time . . . not if you truly love me, want me . . .

She was dimly conscious, as Chad kicked open the front door, that the drumming rain had ceased as abruptly as if shut off like a tap, and already she could hear the chirping of the birds in the dripping branches. Then, incredibly just as they were entering the house, the sun burst out of the dark clouds.

Chad set her down in the middle of the living-room floor and stood back a moment, his wet hands resting on her shoulders, his eyes smouldering with an emotion that caused her throat to constrict. 'You might as well take off that dress,' he said, and she heard the thickness in his voice. 'It's not hiding anything.' He reached out to touch the tip of her breast, which was tantalisingly prominent through the taut wet fabric.

She felt an exquisite throb through her body at his touch. 'Your clothes aren't hiding too much, either,' she retorted huskily, running her eyes boldly over Chad's muscular body. His soaked shorts and T-shirt were moulded to his powerful body like a second skin, revealing sinews and contours that made her blood pound wildly in her ears and chest.

'Is that so? Then I suggest we do something about it.'

Again their eyes met . . . met , and locked. Mesmerised, Gemma found herself wriggling out of her sodden dress, watching Chad watch *her*. She felt no shyness. Even when Chad started removing his own wet clothes, she didn't avert her gaze. She loved him, and she needed him . . . and she wanted him to know it.

She saw the passion burning in his eyes as she stood naked beneath his gaze . . . felt her own body responding to the sight of his, her breasts aching for his touch, her nipples hardening with anticipation.

Next moment his damp body was crushing hers, and as she groaned with pleasure Chad eased her gently down on to the rug. They rolled over and over, savouring the sensation of each other's bodies, their hearts thudding in unison, their mouths showering kisses, their hands clawing wildly at each other, digging into the smooth, damp flesh.

'Gemma . . . I love you!' Chad's voice was husky in her ear.

Her heart soared. 'Oh, Chad, I love you too,' she breathed. She couldn't say more because Chad's open mouth had captured hers, and he was kissing her with a savage intensity that sent tiny explosive waves rocketing through her. She returned his kiss with equal abandon, her mouth moving feverishly under his, her fingers sliding through his hair, while a tight, coiling need built up inside her, screaming to be released.

Still kissing her, Chad rolled her on to her back, letting his hands slide over her silken stomach and down her thighs. It was exquisite torture, causing her to arch compulsively against him, gasping with ecstasy, and longing.

'Gemma . . .' Chad jerked back his head. He was breathing heavily, and his eyes, swimming above hers, were glazed with passion. 'If I go any further I won't be able to stop. Tell me now if you want to wait until our wedding night . . .'

Wedding night! Hazily, through her whirling passion, she felt a leaping joy in her heart.

'I want you, Chad . . . now,' she whispered. 'Please . . . don't stop now.'

'Gemma . . . my darling . . . my love!' He buried his lips in the creamy hollow of her throat, and she felt the increased urgency of his hands on her body, her breasts, her stomach, until gusts of desire began to shake her and, shuddering in response, Chad lowered his hot, moist body over hers. As the turbulence of his passion swirled around her, she writhed beneath him, a cry bursting from her lips as she felt herself hurtling to blissful, intoxicating heights she had previously only dreamed about. As she floated into a glorious oblivion, she felt Chad give an explosive shudder, and become still.

Afterwards, as they lay drowsily satisfied in each other's arms, they talked.

'I wish I could have found you last night.' Gemma sighed, peering up into Chad's face. 'I was devastated when I found your boat had gone. I—I thought you'd turned away from me—for good. That you didn't care whether I stayed or not.'

He stirred in her arms, admitting wryly, 'It was pure self-preservation, my love. I thought you had turned away from *me,* because you'd succeeded in getting what you had wanted all along—Jonathan *and* your Sydney practice. I decided to spend the night on my boat instead of going home. On my way to the marina I ran into Melanie, and I ended up taking her to the mainland to spend the night with her mother. I stayed on board, thinking about *you,* my darling. Thinking I'd lost you. We sailed back this morning in time for surgery.'

Gemma felt a stab of remorse. Such a simple explanation. She should have known!

'And Melanie visited you after surgery this morning to see how her portrait was going.' She didn't even bother to make it into a question. It seemed so clear now.

Chad looked down at her, his expression probing, bemused. 'Right first time. You didn't think it was for any other reason, by any chance?' A knowing, teasing light was dawning in his eye.

'Oh, Chad, I've been such a fool!' She felt so ashamed. He deserved to know what a jealous idiot she had been. 'I thought you and Melanie . . . She—she'd told me how lonely she was, with Nick away so often. And—and someone told me you'd gone off together last night . . .' She stopped, flushing furiously.

Chad stared at her, looking more amused than shocked or angry. 'What a duffer you are,' he said mildly. 'I don't play around with the wives of my friends . . . or with my nurses. Or with my patients, either. You should know that.'

Her flush deepened. 'I know that *now*,' she said in a muffled voice. 'I was hurt when I found you'd gone and I—I jumped to conclusions. I didn't want to believe it, but—but when I saw Melanie leaving here just now . . . Oh, Chad, I thought you didn't care for me . . . that even if you did, you wouldn't want to make a permanent commitment, after—after being married unhappily once. I—I thought that was why you had turned away from me. Particularly now that you knew I was a doctor . . .'

Now he did look shocked. 'I turned away because I was sure you would take Jonathan back . . . now that he'd given in. I guess that makes me a fool too,' he said, tenderly tracing her cheek with his finger. 'I thought you'd been secretly hankering after him all along. That was all I cared about. Not the fact that you were a doctor.'

She felt a rush of emotion. 'I came after you last night,' she told him with a shake of her head, 'to tell you that I had made up my mind to stay up north—with you, if you wanted me. I don't want Jonathan—or the Sydney practice. I want *you,* Chad. Only you.'

Chad ran his fingers through her hair, brushing the silken strands away from her face, before answering.

When he did, his tone was serious. 'I'm relieved to hear that you don't want Jonathan, of course. But I would never ask you to give up your career, my darling. I'll come to Sydney with you and find work there, so that you *can* accept the parnership you've been offered . . .'

She looked at him with wondering eyes. 'Chad, how can you make such an offer? Such a sacrifice! You know what it did to your marriage with Roxanne . . . having a full-time working wife.'

'That wasn't what killed our marriage—Roxanne and I were poles apart in too many ways. There was no sharing—and far too little caring, let alone love. It will be different with us . . . we share so many things. The same interests, the same sense of humour, the same outlook on life, the same dedication to medicine. And we love each other . . .' He stroked her cheek with his knuckles. His eyes were soft, aglow with the love he spoke of. 'And our love will grow and grow,' he murmured softly. 'And when we have children, we'll love them too.'

'Oh, Chad.' She was so overcome, she could hardly speak. 'I feel just the same about you . . . It was so different with Jonathan. I was selfish . . . stubborn . . . I thought only of what *I* wanted. I wasn't prepared to make compromises because I didn't love him enough to want to work things out to our *mutual* satisfaction. Chad, I'd give up everything for you . . . go anywhere . . . I'll do whatever you want me to do. I'll work as little or as much as you want . . . just so long as we're together.' She could hardly believe she was uttering the words she had earlier rehearsed in her mind, words that only this morning she had thought she would never have a chance to say to Chad's face.

She saw the love burning in his eyes. 'I'd never ask you

to give up anything,' he said softly. 'Let alone make demands. There won't be any laying down of laws . . . You and I will sit down very soon and we'll work out *together* what we intend to do . . . whether we stay up here in Queensland, or whether we go down to Sydney. Whether we work separately or go into practice together. Now there's a thought . . .' He paused, his eyes contemplative. 'I rather fancy that idea . . .'

'Are you laying down the law, Dr Rivers?' she asked teasingly.

'Merely one of the options open to us,' he said, drawing her back into his arms. 'Whatever we decide, we'll decide together . . . and whatever our decision is, it will be something we can both share, that will bring us even closer together. And when we've decided, we'll go and tell my mother . . . *together*.'

'Chad, do you mean it?' Joy and relief lit up her face.

'Don't I always say what I mean?' His lips brushed hers. 'If my mother is to become a grandmother in the not too distant future, I'd like her to get to know her daughter-in-law first.'

'And her son,' Gemma suggested gently, her words muffled by his lips.

'And her son,' he agreed, before his mouth stifled any further talk between them.

HARLEQUIN
Romance

Coming Next Month

#3037 DARK MEMORIES Kerry Allyne
Teal's love for Dare lay in the past. Now a capable career woman, she's in control of her own life and feelings. So why, when it's only business, should she feel nervous about meeting him again...?

#3038 A LITTLE BIT COUNTRY Debbie Macomber
Can a city girl find happiness with a "country man"? Yes—except that Clay Franklin, the rancher Rorie's fallen in love with, is engaged to someone else. Someone neither he nor Rorie wants to hurt....

#3039 IMPULSIVE PROPOSAL Jeneth Murrey
Ellis never told Gideon her real reason for marrying Robert. Now, returning to her Welsh home after Robert's death, she realizes that for little Davey's sake, Gideon will have to know the truth—and that she'll enjoy telling him.

#3040 RUMOR HAS IT Celia Scott
As the rumors about Lucinda and "her Englishman" flourish, so does Lucinda. But her newfound confidence doesn't prepare her for Leo Grosvenor's surprise return, nor for his more surprising proposal.

#3041 FAREWELL TO LOVE Jessica Steele
Meredith has been swept off her feet, and for her it's love at first sight. She assumes that Ryan Carlile feels the same way about her. Then her dream is abruptly shattered on their wedding day.

#3042 THE MAXTON BEQUEST Alison York
For the first time in her life, Ros feels as though she has a home. Then Dan Maxton appears, handsome and charming, and assumes that money can buy anything. And he wants to turn Ros's world upside down....

Available in March wherever paperback books are sold, or through Harlequin Reader Service:

In the U.S.
901 Fuhrmann Blvd.
P.O. Box 1397
Buffalo, N.Y. 14240-1397

In Canada
P.O. Box 603
Fort Erie, Ontario
L2A 5X3

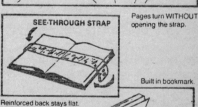
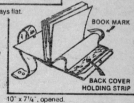

HARLEQUIN Temptation

The Pirate
JAYNE ANN KRENTZ

At the heart of every powerful romance story lies a legend. There are many romantic legends and countless modern variations on them, but they all have one thing in common: They are tales of brave, resourceful women who must gentle and tame the powerful, passionate men who are their true mates.

The enormous appeal of Jayne Ann Krentz lies in her ability to create modern-day versions of these classic romantic myths, and her LADIES AND LEGENDS trilogy showcases this talent. Believing that a storyteller who can bring legends to life deserves special attention, Harlequin has chosen the first book of the trilogy—THE PIRATE—to receive our Award of Excellence. Look for it now.

AE-PIR-1A